KT-489-434

THE LONDON BOROUGH
www.bromley.gov.uk

Mottingham Library
020 8857 5406   05/19

Please return/renew this item
by the last date shown.
Books may also be renewed by
phone and Internet.

Tel: (0116) 246 4515
website: www.foundation-live-search.com

GIRL MEETS BODY

Reunited with his English war bride,
Sybil, after two years, Tim takes her back
to the USA with him — but where to
live, in the middle of the post-World
War II housing crisis? They meet a
friend of Sybil's deceased father, who
promises to help. Next thing they know,
the New Jersey chapter of the British-
American War Brides Improvement
Association arranges accommodation
for them in the isolated coastal community of Merry Point. Here they meet
their curmudgeonly landlord and an
inept handyman. Then Sybil finds a
body on the pier . . .

JACK IAMS

◆

GIRL MEETS BODY

Complete and Unabridged

LINFORD
Leicester

First published in Great Britain

First Linford Edition
published 2016

A catalogue record for this book is available
from the British Library.

ISBN 978–1–4448–2878–8

Published by
F. A. Thorpe (Publishing)
Anstey, Leicestershire

Set by Words & Graphics Ltd.
Anstey, Leicestershire
Printed and bound in Great Britain by
T. J. International Ltd., Padstow, Cornwall

This book is printed on acid-free paper

1

Do Not Disturb

Tim Ludlow's war bride, the former Sybil Hastings of London, poked her head into the bathroom of their hotel suite. 'There's a tap marked *ice water*,' she said. 'There really is.' Tim heard a squish. 'And it really is ice water, too. For dousing the head, I suppose, on bad mornings.'

'Most people just drink it,' said Tim.

'Oh,' said Sybil. She wandered back into the austere pink and green sitting room. Its windows, between stiff draperies, were blurred and gray with the late October drizzle. 'Darling,' she said, 'would you think me frightfully ungrateful if I suggested that ice water is the last thing in the world I feel like drinking?'

'There was supposed to be something else,' said Tim. He looked at his watch and made a fidgety move toward the phone. Soft footsteps and a cheerful clinking sounded just then in the corridor, followed by a discreet knock. 'Here we are,' said Tim with relief. 'Come in.'

A bell-hop, grinning like a bell-hop in an ad, pushed a wagon into the room. Pale goblets trembled on it beside a sweating silver bucket.

'Tim, darling!' cried Sybil. 'Champagne! There's nothing in the world I like better!'

'Nothing?' said Tim.

She gave him a mocking glance. 'Well, there's bridge.' Then her dark eyes widened. 'Blimey, I've married you without asking if you play bridge.'

'The registrar asked me.'

'What did you say?'

'Same thing I said to the rest of his questions. I do.'

'Thank God,' sighed Sybil. 'I've always thought the ceremony should include something about never taking this, thy partner, out of business doubles.'

The bell-hop cleared his throat. 'Where'll I put this?' he asked.

'Oh, anywhere,' said Tim.

'Anywhere indeed!' said Sybil. 'Wheel it into the bedroom, laddie.'

The bell-hop's grin grew broader, almost, thought Tim, to the point of impertinence. He wheeled it in, and on his way out, Tim handed him a dollar.

Tim stared at the bedroom door, which Sybil had closed. Should he wait, or knock, or barge in, or what? He wasn't very sure about anything. It was more than two years since he had seen Sybil, and this day, to which he had so long looked forward, had brought with it a sudden sense of uncertainty. There had been hours of waiting on the chill, damp pier for the bride ship — a callous phrase, like cattle-boat, yet pagan and exciting, too. There had been the palaver with customs and newspapermen that shattered the emotional intensity of meeting. Together at last in a taxicab, they had listened through one rain-dreary street after another to a discourse by the driver on the merits of Notre Dame. ('Is he talking about priests?' Sybil had whispered. 'Neophytes,' said Tim.)

Even during their first few minutes alone in the hotel, Tim continued to feel much as he once had when a German colonel unexpectedly surrendered to him. However, things had worked out all right on that occasion, and he hoped and trusted that they would again.

'Tim, sweet,' called Sybil from the bedroom, 'have you seen my medal?'

'No,' said Tim, frowning at what struck him as an incongruous subject. 'I didn't even know you had a medal.'

'I got it for driving you around. Come in and see it. I have it on.'

'All right,' said Tim.

'Incidentally,' she added, 'it's *all* I have on.'

Tim gulped and took a quick, happy look at himself in the mirror. He straightened his tie. 'I hope it's not the kind that pins on,' he said and went into the bedroom.

★ ★ ★

Tim and Sybil didn't really know each other awfully well. For the first few weeks of their acquaintance, she had been one of several trim and efficient young ATS drivers assigned to a group of officers, including Tim, in the American Army's Division of Monuments, Fine Arts, and Archives, which was then waiting nervously for the invasion to open up its task on the Continent. Like Tim, who had been an instructor at a midwestern college, most of them had emerged, blinking, from the ordered tranquility of academic life into the crisp confusion of the Army, only too conscious of how unwarlike they were. Among the ATS drivers, Sybil told Tim afterward, they were known as the Panzer Professors.

One night in May, Sybil was driving Tim to his quarters from an officers' club off Grosvenor Square when a buzz bomb cut out directly overhead. In the moment of terrible silence that followed, when the wet, green smell of spring was sweeter than it had ever been before, Sybil turned suddenly toward the back seat and said, 'Hold my hand, Captain. It's going to be close.'

Even as he took her hand in his own, which was shaking as if it held dice, the earth exploded and, less than a hundred yards away, a geyser of debris rose and

5

slowly fell, a good deal of it over the car. It was strangely soft debris. The bomb had landed among the flowerbeds of St. James's Park.

'Jolly lucky hit, that,' murmured Sybil. 'For us, I mean. Poor show for Jerry.'

Then she realized he was holding her hand and withdrew it. 'Sorry about the display of nerves,' she said.

Tim tried to say something suitable, but his voice was missing. He was trembling still, and conscious of very little outside of two facts: he was alive, and his driver's face in the unreal moonlight was white and beautiful. He leaned forward and kissed her.

'Captain!' exclaimed Sybil, but she didn't sound angry. 'I believe that's forbidden by the Articles of War.'

Tim's voice came back. 'Damn the Articles of War,' he said and kissed her again. In the distance, harsh and welcome, the all-clear sounded.

'Shall we be off, sir?' asked Sybil briskly.

'No,' said Tim. He leaned halfway across the back of the seat and took what he could reach of her in his arms. It occurred to him, dimly and unimportantly, that he must be presenting quite a spectacle to anyone approaching from the rear.

It also occurred to him, after he had gone to bed, that the only conversation he had contributed to the most romantic interlude of his life thus far had been a disrespectful reference to the Articles of War.

A few days later, on D-Day Minus One as it turned out, they were married at Paddington Registry Office. A week after that, a week during which he scarcely saw his bride, he got his orders for the Continent.

'Are you scared, darling?' Sybil asked the night before he left.

'Not of the enemy,' said Tim. 'I probably won't be anywhere near the enemy. But I'm scared of the American generals I'm supposed to keep from shelling cathedrals. Can you imagine me telling General Patton he's got to change his line of fire?'

'Of course,' said Sybil. 'Why should

you be more scared of a general than I, a lance corporal, am of a captain?'

'I don't expect to be in bed with any generals,' said Tim.

It was their last night together for a long, long time. Tim followed the armies through France and Luxemburg and into Germany, where the task of searching out and restoring the works of art picked up here and there by Hermann Goering and fellow connoisseurs lengthened past one V-Day and then another, deep into the turbulent months of peace.

For a lover of art, it was exhilarating work. To stumble unexpectedly upon a cache of Rubenses and Rembrandts gave Tim much the same sensation that a man of coarser tastes might have derived from stumbling into the Goldwyn Girls' dressing room.

But even when the excitement of the job was at its peak, the edges of his mind were frayed with loneliness for Sybil. Later on, when the work settled down to the humdrum business of sorting, cataloguing, storting, and shipping, his longing for her turned into a constant ache. More tantalizing than the actual separation was the fact that he scarcely knew, and had scarcely loved, his wife. His colleagues, most of whom were older than his twenty-nine years, all seemed to have placid spouses who sat on American porches waiting for them and sending them snapshots of the children. Whereas Sybil was a figment of a dream, something he sometimes wasn't sure had really happened.

She wrote to him, of course, but her letters, telling of her life among friends he had never met, against unfamiliar backgrounds, heightened his sense of distance. They gave him that feeling of disquiet that sensitive children get when they first realize their parents' lives don't center around the nursery.

His own parents wrote, too, of course. Between congratulatory lines lurked midwestern suspicion of the foreign. What about her family, they wanted to know. And there wasn't much he could tell them. All Sybil had ever mentioned was that she didn't remember her mother, and her father had died just before the war started. There hadn't been room for family discussions in the time at his and Sybil's disposal. There had barely been room to eat. He had a notion that she came of genteel, possibly elegant, folk, but it didn't bother him one way or the other when he was with her. Now, once in a while, it bothered him.

A thoughtful friend sent him an editorial from a Chicago newspaper, deploring overseas marriages. *Ninety percent of these girls*, it said right there in print, *are out for what they can get*. Tim utilized the editorial in the most fitting way, but sometimes, on sleepless nights, it would creep into his mind like a singing commercial and he would find himself brooding on possibilities that two minutes of Sybil's companionship would have blown out of the window.

Months dragged on. When he was finally released, he happened to be in the Tyrol, and the simplest way home lay through Italy. He pulled all the wires he could to manage it via England, but he might as well have pulled dandelions. None of the Army's channels led to England.

10

So it was that two and a half years after his marriage, he found himself in a New York hotel room with a tall, pale, intensely desirable stranger. He had a feeling the house detective might knock at any minute.

2

Not Even a Haystack

'Any champagne left?' asked Sybil.

'A spot,' said Tim. He lifted the bottle out of the now-melted ice and poured the faintly fizzing remains into goblets. Sybil thrust a bare arm from beneath the green quilt and raised the glass toward him.

'Here's to reunion,' she said.

'Here's to it.'

'Almost worth the separation.'

'Well, no.'

'I said 'almost.''

She smiled over the rim of the glass. Her face and shoulders were creamy white above the green covering, against the duller white of the pillows. It was a face that might have been of classic beauty if the nose hadn't been a touch too short, the mouth a shade too rounded, the eyes much too mischievous. As for her hair, it was smoothly dark, although in tumbled disorder at the moment. She pushed it back as she sipped her champagne.

Tim sipped his, too. He felt fine, so fine that he almost forgot about the bad news he had for her. He was sitting on the foot of the bed with a gray Army bathrobe draped around his lanky frame. He had a long, lean face, which had been sun-burned and hardened by the past few years, and which in repose was solemn. When he grinned, though, the solemnity turned into a pleasant boyishness, better suited to his always-rumpled brown hair.

'Well, Mrs. L,' he said, 'how do you like the United States?'

'Is that where I am? All I know is that I'm with you. That's all I want to know.'

Tim was smiling, but there was an anxious little wrinkle in his forehead. 'I hope that's true,' he said. 'It'll make things easier.'

'What sort of things? Maybe I spoke too soon.'

Tim swallowed. 'Housing. We've no place to live.'

'Oh,' said Sybil. 'I thought you meant

13

we were going to jail together or something of that sort.'

'We'd be better off in jail.'

'Don't be gloomy, darling. With you, I'd live in a haystack.'

'A vacant haystack,' said Tim, 'would be harder to find than a needle inside one. You'd have to buy the needle, too.'

'Then why don't we stay right here? Right here in bed.'

'We can. For five days.'

'They'd be five lovely days,' said Sybil dreamily. 'Something to look back on.'

'No doubt,' said Tim, 'but I don't want to look back on them from a park bench.'

Sybil sat up. 'Oh, dear,' she said, 'I suppose we've got to be serious about this.'

'Yes,' said Tim, 'and you're not helping matters by popping out from under that quilt. Get back.'

'All right,' she said, slipping lazily back onto the pillows, 'let's be serious. To begin with, where is it we can't find a place to live?'

'Nowhere. Anywhere. It doesn't much matter.'

14

'But don't you have to be near that college in the midlands where you teach children to put mustaches on the Mona Lisa?'

'Midwest, not midlands. And we needn't live there if we don't want to.'

'Lumme,' said Sybil, 'I've either married into the unemployed or the idle rich.'

'It's like this,' said Tim. 'I could go back to my old teaching job tomorrow if I wanted to, but even there the housing situation is murder. And even if we could find a wigwam out there, I'd still be a lowly instructor. Which, financially speaking, is very, very lowly. On the other hand, if between now and next fall I can wangle myself a Ph.D., I'd stand a pretty fair chance of landing an assistant professorship someplace.'

'Would I have to call you Doctor?'

'Oh, sure. But you got used to calling me Captain, didn't you?'

'More or less. How does one go about wangling a Ph.D.? Is there a black market in them?'

'Probably. However, I propose to go through the usual procedure of writing a

15

dissertation. Something hefty. The fallacy of nationalism in art, something like that.'

'Most impressive,' said Sybil. 'Shall I help you?'

'Yes. But not with no clothes on.'

'Tsk, tsk. Double negative. And from a man about to write a Ph.D. thesis, too.'

'In order to write this thesis, aside from grammar,' said Tim, 'I'll need a desk with a roof over it. What I'd like would be someplace in the country, not too far from a city or at least from a public library. But try and find it.'

'Even if we did find it,' said Sybil, 'how would we eat? I hate to be mercenary, but I've been doing some awfully slim eating the last few years.'

Tim grinned. 'I've got three months' terminal leave pay and a couple of penny banks I managed to fill before the war. That ought to see us through the thesis, at least. Afterward, maybe we'll wind up in a nice little house on the edge of some college campus with built-in bookcases and an open fireplace.'

'And I'll have other professors' wives to tea and flirt with the undergraduates.'

16

'Any undergraduate caught flirting with you,' said Tim, 'will be automatically flunked.'

'Gracious,' said Sybil, 'that sounds dreadful. Do you do it with a cat-o'-nine-tails?'

'It depends. But let's not dwell on the rosy future. The question before the meeting is, do we dwell at all?'

'So what do we do about it? Aside from lying in bed and drinking champagne. Not that I'm complaining, mind you.'

'Well,' said Tim, 'I've got a car. Not much of a car, but a car.'

'But darling,' cried Sybil, sitting up again, 'how marvelous! You know, people in England don't just have cars. Cars impress us the way titles do you. And they're much more useful.'

'And much easier to pick up second-hand.'

'Possibly. So we have a car. How thrilling. And what do we do with it?'

'Well, I thought we might drive around the country for a few days and see what we can find in the way of a desk and a roof. Anyway, that's the plan.'

'Lovely. When do we start?'

'Whenever you like. I thought it might be fun to have an evening on the town first.'

'Oh, wonderful. A real bang-up binge.'

'Why not? A fellow doesn't meet a new wife every day.'

3

Double Feature with Fireworks

Their evening on the town started at the Stork Club in order to get that orthodox procedure out of the way. They drank a dry martini each and saw Walter Winchell's very own table. 'Like Dr. Johnson's at the Cheshire Cheese,' said Sybil. Then, for a change of pace, they looked in at Tim Costello's on Third Avenue and saw James Thurber's very own drawings on the wall. 'Like Tom Webster's at the Falstaff,' said Sybil. They had dinner at a little French restaurant where they held hands and ate Crêpes Suzette. 'Like Prunier's,' said Sybil. Afterward there were night clubs: Larue, which reminded Sybil of Quaglino's; Leon and Eddie's, which reminded her of the Palladium Crazy Gang; and finally the Downtown Café Society.

'What does this remind you of?' asked

Tim, watching Meade Lux Lewis take a piano apart.

'Nothing on earth,' said Sybil.

'I thought not,' said Tim. 'It's supposed to be out of this world.'

At three in the morning, this bit of badinage sounded a great deal funnier than it would have at three in the afternoon. It even sounded funny to another couple standing next to them at the crowded bar, and presently they were buying each other drinks. It seemed perfectly natural, as the music and the lights faded, for the other couple to suggest that they all go on together to the Breeze Club.

Tim looked dubious, but Sybil cried rapturously, 'The Breeze Club! Why, even in London we've heard of that. Something like the old Four Hundred.'

The other couple didn't know anything about the old Four Hundred, but the Breeze Club was one swell place, they said. Open till noon.

'Don't you have to be known to get in?' asked Tim.

Sure, but that was all right, the other

couple was known. Next thing, the four of them were in a taxi, bowling north. It was a long ride to the Breeze Club, which was way uptown on the East River, and a damp and chilly ride as well. Tim felt himself growing soberer and soberer, not to mention sleepier, and the whole enterprise growing less and less attractive. Still, Sybil seemed to be enjoying herself enormously, and he decided he owed her all the fun that could be squeezed out of this one night.

'Tim, darling,' said Sybil, 'stop yawning.'

The Breeze Club was packed and confusing. Getting into it was confusing to begin with, because you entered at street level and then went down in a satin-lined elevator. The place got its name, presumably, from its site at the river's edge, but there was no breeze in evidence. In fact, a breeze could hardly have fought its way through the atmosphere, cloyed with perfume and opaque with smoke. Tim began to feel woozy as soon as they got inside. He had a dizzying sensation of being swallowed up in the milling, chattering crowd, mostly in evening dress. Who were all these people, he wondered, who wanted to stay up till noon?

'Oh, look,' exclaimed Sybil, pointing toward an adjoining room, its doorway hung in heavy crimson. 'Roulette! I adore roulette.'

'Better not adore it tonight,' said Tim. 'We're almost broke.'

Sybil didn't seem to hear him. She was staring with wide, excited eyes at the crowded roulette table. Then she turned to him and said, 'I've got to spend a penny first. I'll meet you at the bar.'

She slipped away into the crowd, leaving him with a sudden sense of panic lest he lose her. He looked around for the other couple, but they apparently had seen some people they knew and drifted off. A drink, he thought, might help him shake off this feeling of being on the edge of a maelstrom, and he threaded his way to the bar. The bartender fixed him a Scotch and soda, picked up the dollar Tim laid on the wet mahogany and said, 'Thanks for the tip. The drink'll be two fifty.'

Tim sipped the whisky, trying to get his money's worth of pleasure out of it, and stared across the room, wondering from what direction Sybil would come. Then he saw her and blinked. She was carrying something, something decidedly large. For a second it looked like a coffin, then it looked like a door. It was a door, he discovered as he hurried toward her; a green-painted, slotted wooden door.

'Look at this bloody thing,' said Sybil. 'Absolute gimcrack.'

'I'm sure it is, dear,' said Tim in bewilderment, 'but why have you got it?'

'I wanted to show it to you.'

'Why?'

'Because I seem to have broken it, and she wants ten dollars for it.'

'Who wants ten dollars for it?'

'She does.'

For the first time Tim was aware of somebody chirping at his elbow. It was a woman, small and middle-aged, who might have looked motherly in different circumstances. Just then, she looked step-motherly.

'She walks right into the powder room,

she does,' this small woman was saying, 'and rips this door right off its hinges.'

'They open the other way in England,' said Sybil.

'I don't care how they open in England,' said the small woman. 'How would you feel, mister, if somebody walked into *your* powder room and tore a door right off its hinges?'

'I'd remind myself that the customer is always right,' said Tim.

'You'd expect the customer to pay, though, wouldn't you, right or wrong?'

'Right or wrong, my customer,' said Tim.

'Anyway,' interrupted Sybil, 'you wouldn't expect the customer to pay ten dollars. Not for a bit of gingerbread like this. I offered her two. All I had.'

'All you had?' repeated Tim. 'In that case, I'm afraid — '

'Hey, what the hell's going on here?' snapped a voice behind him. Tim turned and saw a tall, broad-shouldered man in a tightly stretched dinner jacket, a man with blue-black jowls and no forehead to speak of.

24

Sybil said coldly, 'Careful of your language, fellow.'

The big man blinked as if she had struck him on the chin with a fan. His thick lips curled slightly. 'I said what the hell's going on, and that's what I mean.'

The small woman started to explain. 'Okay, pay the ten bucks,' said the big man, 'and then get your ass the hell out of here.

He didn't expect the stinging slap that Sybil planted on his blue-black cheek. He took a dazed step backward, then hunched toward her like an enraged great ape. Tim grabbed at his arm. Under the soft sleeve it felt like an iron bar.

Another voice, to Tim's frank relief, joined the colloquy. 'Easy, Jake,' said the new voice. It belonged to a short, cheerful man in his fifties, with smooth gray hair, a clipped gray mustache, and alert blue eyes. Unlike Jake, he wore his evening clothes as if he were used to them and liked them.

Jake didn't turn immediately. He looked as if he might be counting to ten, then he looked around with a petulant expression. 'Okay,' he said, 'but you know the powder room's a concession and I can't afford no trouble over it.'

'The difficulty with Jake,' the gray-haired man said pleasantly to Tim and Sybil, 'is that he can't get it through his Neanderthal skull that his clientele includes ladies and gentlemen.'

'Ladies!' said Jake. 'Did you see her sock me?'

'Ladies can be quite as high-spirited, Jake, as the trolls you associate with. This particular lady, unless I'm much mistaken, spells it with a capital L.' He smiled at Sybil and said, 'You are the Lady Sybil Hastings, are you not?'

Tim blinked at the gray-haired man and then at Sybil. Sybil was blinking, too; then a slow, almost sheepish smile crossed her face. 'Well, yes,' she said, 'but I've tried awfully hard to live it down. The Lady part, I mean.'

Tim gaped. 'For Pete's sake,' he said, 'why didn't you tell me?'

Sybil shrugged. 'Nonessential,' she said. 'And a lot of rot into the bargain. In any event,' she went on, turning back to the gray-haired man, 'I'm Mrs. Tim Ludlow now. This is Mr. Tim Ludlow.'

'Charmed,' said the gray-haired man.

'But how in the world did you know?' asked Sybil. 'Do you read *Tatler*?'

'Occasionally. It so happens, however, that I had the pleasure of meeting you a good many years ago, when you hadn't been long out of pigtails. It was on a Mediterranean cruise. Remember?'

'Of course I remember,' cried Sybil. 'And now I remember you. You were the jolly American who used to play bridge with Daddy.'

'Quite so. I might add that I was extremely fond of — of the late Earl.' He lowered his voice a trifle. 'His death was a severe blow to me.'

He and Sybil were both silent for a moment, while Tim stared from one to the other.

Then the gray-haired man, speaking more cheerfully, as if to indicate that the solemnities had been duly observed, said, 'I must confess that I had the advantage of you. There was a bit in this morning's paper about you and your fellow brides' arrival. Or should I say sister-brides?'

'Sisters under the skin,' said Sybil.

The gray-haired man smiled. 'It occurred to me,' he went on, 'that you might possibly appear in this checkered establishment. Your father was a great one for the old Four Hundred Club, and this is its nearest New York equivalent.'

'Tim, darling,' said Sybil, 'this is something wonderful. More wonderful than you dream. I propose we observe the occasion with a bottle of bubbly.'

Tim coughed. 'There's a slight technical hitch,' he said, looking embarrassed.

'I'm sure this kind chap will cash a check for you,' said Sybil, waving airily toward Jake. The latter's eyebrows rose into his hair's oily gloss.

The gray-haired man held up a restraining hand. 'I quite agree,' he said, 'that the occasion calls for champagne, but let there be no misunderstanding as to whose treat it shall be. Jake, send a bottle of Cordon Rouge to my table. Preferably the twenty-eight.'

'What about my door?' demanded a querulous little voice.

'Imagine forgetting that one's holding a door,' said Sybil merrily. 'Here it is, duck.'

The woman accepted it and said, 'Yes, but — '

'Pother,' interrupted the gray-haired man sharply. 'Get thee back to your nunnery. This way, good people.'

He led them through the crowd, like Moses passing through the Red Sea, to a low balcony that extended along one side of the room. There was a vacant table at one end, toward which their host bowed them. It was comparatively cool and tranquil on the balcony, and one could look down upon the kaleidoscopic crowd with Olympian detachment.

'Reminds me of the Café Royal balcony on extension night,' said Sybil.

'Just so,' said the gray-haired man. 'Much the same sort of people, too. Stage folk, artists, a dash of society, journalists, and the like. What you might call the moneyed Bohemia.'

'If I'm not being personal,' said Tim, 'are you the owner?'

The other shook his head with rueful amusement. 'I've paid for it several times over,' he said. 'I'm just a very, very good customer. Incidentally, I haven't introduced myself properly, have I? My name is Magruder. Sam Magruder.'

'Of course,' exclaimed Sybil. 'It's coming back to me now. I've often heard Daddy speak of you.'

Magruder smiled reminiscently. 'You and I must have a long talk one of these days. I'm sure Mr. Ludlow won't mind — although, of course, he's more than welcome to join us.'

'I never butt in on old home weeks,' said Tim.

Magruder felt in his pockets. 'Afraid I haven't a card,' he apologized. 'I'll scribble my number down for you.' He brought out a black notebook and started to write in it. 'By the way,' he said, 'you'd better give me your address, too.'

'I'm afraid we haven't one,' said Sybil. 'Except for a frightfully temporary hotel.'

'What!' exclaimed Magruder, looking up from the notebook. 'You mean you've no place to live?'

'That's how it looks,' said Tim.

Magruder laid down his fountain pen

and stared at both of them with genuine concern. 'By George,' he said, 'this is terrible. Is this the sort of hospitality America gives its English visitors? Is this the thanks our veterans get? By George, something's going to be done about this.'

'I wish it were,' sighed Tim.

'Damn it, young man, I'm serious. Something will be done. As sure as my name's Sam Magruder.' He gave his head a firm little shake. Then he wrote some more in the notebook, ripped the page out, and handed it to Sybil. She tucked it into her bag.

It struck Tim that their host must have written a good deal more than his telephone number, a thought which Magruder apparently read because he chuckled and said, 'I've added a few protestations of undying love. D'you mind?'

'Not a bit,' said Tim, immediately ashamed of any unworthy suspicion. 'Me, I've got my eye on that redhead over there.'

'Redhead?' said Magruder, looking. 'I don't see any redhead.'

'I'm afraid she's imaginary,' said Tim. 'Strictly a dream girl.'

Magruder, still looking across the big room, started to laugh, then the laugh died on his lips. They tightened and his blue eyes turned hard and glittery.

'What's the matter?' asked Sybil. She and Tim both turned in the direction of his gaze and saw a group of men coming through the red-curtained entrance. They were in dinner jackets, but kept their hats on. The hats looked more natural than the dinner jackets.

'Coppers?' asked Sybil.

'No,' said Magruder. For another second or two, he remained immobile, as if fascinated by a cobra's eye; then swiftly, without rising, he slipped from his chair and moved in a crouching run toward the wall beyond the table. There was a door there, painted like the wall, and Magruder pushed it a little way open. 'Better come with me,' he whispered. 'That's what your father'd have wanted. Both of you. And keep down.'

'Come on,' said Sybil to Tim. She slithered from the table to the door, which Magruder pushed further open for her. Tim followed into a narrow stone passageway, dimly lit and damp, and Magruder followed him, pulling the door shut.

Even as the latch clicked, a sharp, dry crack sounded in the room behind them, then another and another, each followed instantly by a splintering thud against the door.

'My God,' said Tim, 'those were shots.'

'Isn't it exciting?' said Sybil. 'I'm crazy about New York.'

'Better let me go first,' said Magruder. 'And don't dawdle.' He slid past them and they trailed him through the gloom.

Three more shots crackled distantly beyond the stone walls, and somebody screamed; it might have been a man or a woman.

'Watch it,' called Magruder over his shoulder. 'Flight of steps ahead.'

They could see his head and shoulders descending. Tim took Sybil's arm and said, 'Careful, honey.'

'I'm all right,' said Sybil. 'Having a lovely time, in fact.'

The steps were steep and uneven, and the dampness sweated more freely from the stones on either side. Below, a patch of light appeared, then the wet and malodorous smell of the East River.

They emerged onto a ledge a few feet above the water, darkly visible through the mists of breaking dawn. Beside them, a smooth wall rose endlessly into the lightening sky.

'This way,' called Magruder, moving along the ledge with easy caution. 'Don't be alarmed by this stuff around you. It's only daylight.' He sounded exhilarated.

'Reminds me of the sewers of Paris,' said Sybil.

'Reminds me of a double feature,' said Tim.

Magruder halted a little distance ahead of them. As they caught up, Tim saw that he was standing at the foot of another flight of steps cut into the wall. 'These'll take you up to the street,' he said. 'There's a cab stand a block north. Forgive me if I don't accompany you, but it's a bit of a climb for a chap of my age and habits.'

'But what are you going to do?' asked Sybil anxiously.

'Watch the sunrise.' He smiled and

patted her shoulder. 'There'll probably be a commotion in the street,' he went on, 'but don't you get mixed up in it. Go straight home. And don't lose my number. I'll be waiting to hear from you.'

He made them a courtly little bow and a careless salute, then he turned and stepped off the ledge. Sybil gasped and clutched at Tim. Neither had seen, in the mist, the small motorboat bumping gently alongside. Magruder stood up in it, waving; then he cast off, and the boat itself vanished in the chill grayness.

'It reminds me of the *Morte d'Arthur*,' said Sybil. 'And if you say anything about double features, I'll push you into the river.'

'Honey,' said Tim, 'you're crying.'

'I know I am,' said Sybil. 'He was a friend of Daddy's.'

As they started up the steps, the dawn was shattered over their heads by the shrieking of a multitude of sirens.

4

War Brides Improved

Sybil opened one eye upon the soupy light of blinds drawn against a gray afternoon. For a moment she wasn't sure where she was. Her gaze moved slowly around the square, impersonal bedroom, then landed on Tim's face, more boyish than ever in rumpled sleep. She smiled and brushed his cheek with her lips, then she sat up and looked at her wristwatch on the bedside table. It was one o'clock, presumably post-meridian. She swung her feet out of bed, wiggled her toes into slippers, got up, and padded into the sitting room. She closed the door.

Her handbag lay on the pink sofa. She opened it and fumbled for the slip of paper Sam Magruder had given her the night before. She unfolded it and read: 'Imperative I see you alone as soon as possible. Strictly alone. Call me at MU8-1239. Don't worry about a place to stay. I'm taking care of it. Watch your step.'

Sybil folded it and slipped it into the monogrammed pocket of her pajama coat. She opened the bedroom door softly, listened a moment, then closed it. She picked up the phone and dialed Magruder's number.

A gruff voice answered, 'Yeah?'

'Is Mr. Magruder there?'

'Wait a minute.' Apparently the voice consulted somebody else because it returned and asked, 'Who wants to know?'

She hesitated. 'Tell him it's Sybil.'

There was another pause for consultation, and Sybil thought she heard somebody laugh. The voice came back and said, 'He ain't here. He's moved away.'

The receiver clicked in her ear. 'Hullo,' she said. 'Are you there?' Only the insulting cackle of the dial tone answered. 'Damn,' she said and put down the phone. She bit her lip and looked out of the window, frowning.

Almost immediately the phone rang. Sybil jumped, then reached for it. A hearty feminine voice with a hint of a Lancashire accent boomed out of it.

'Would this be Mrs. Timothy Ludlow?'

'It would.'

'The former Lady Sybil Hastings?'

'None other.'

The bedroom door opened and Tim poked his head through it, blinking sleepily. 'Thought I heard the phone,' he said. 'Who is it?'

'Don't know yet,' said Sybil.

'This,' went on the hearty voice, 'is the British-American War Bride Improvement Association. BAWBIA, for short. My name is Mrs. Lemuel Barrelforth, President of the New Jersey chapter. Welcome to the United States.'

'Thank you,' said Sybil.

'Who is it?' asked Tim. Sybil shushed him.

'It has been called to our attention,' the voice of Mrs. Lemuel Barrelforth boomed on, 'that you and your veteran husband are without a place to live. In other words, you need improvement. That's what the Association's for.'

'You mean you'll help us find a place?'

'I certainly do. And I'm pretty sure we can.'

38

'But how marvelous!' cried Sybil. 'And how kind!' She paused a moment. 'Was it, by any chance,' she asked, 'a Mr. Magruder who brought us to your attention?'

'The matter was taken up with the Central Welcoming Committee,' replied Mrs. Barrelforth, 'and turned over by them to the New Jersey chapter. New Jersey, you know, is the Garden State, and where there are gardens, there are houses. Stands to reason, doesn't it?'

'I suppose it does,' said Sybil.

'What the heck's this all about?' asked Tim. 'Something about a house?'

Sybil nodded.

'To get down to cases,' Mrs. Barrelforth went on, 'we've already got a house lined up for you. It's got its drawbacks, but it's also got a roof and four walls. Shall I describe it more fully?'

'I think you'd better speak to my husband,' said Sybil.

'Right-o,' said Mrs. Barrelforth. 'Put him on.'

Sybil put her hand over the mouthpiece. 'It's something called the British-American War Brides Improvement Association,' she said to Tim. 'And apparently, they've found us a house.'

'It must be a gag,' said Tim. 'Things like this don't happen.'

'Let's not look it in the mouth,' said Sybil, handing him the phone.

She perched on the arm of the sofa while Tim talked. Or rather, while Tim listened. He said 'Uh-huh' and 'I see' several times while a pleased incredulity gathered on his face. 'Gosh,' he said finally, 'it certainly sounds good to me. Can I call you back . . . ? Oh. Right away, eh? Do you mind hanging on a minute?' He covered the mouthpiece and turned to Sybil, looking dazed but delighted. 'It seems to be on the level,' he said. 'The house is in a place called Merry Point, a seaside resort on the Jersey coast. That's the big drawback.'

'Why?' asked Sybil. 'What's wrong with a seaside resort?'

'Because in winter a Jersey seaside resort is just about as jolly as Wuthering Heights. It'll be bleak, windswept, cold, and lonelier than Mount Everest.'

'We'll have each other,' said Sybil.

40

'I'll do my best to be entertaining,' said Tim. 'Card tricks and so on.'

'Will there be four for bridge?'

'I don't know. From what I gather, the only inhabitants outside of us will be what the summer people call natives.'

'How quaint. Is it far away?' asked Sybil.

'About seventy-five miles. We could go into the city now and again. We'll have the car, and there's a town with a railroad station about five miles away. So we won't be completely cut off.'

'I should think we could stick it,' said Sybil. 'What about the house itself?'

'The house, apparently, is very comfortable. One of these big old-fashioned summer places, with the added advantage of an oil burner.'

'Furnished?'

'Yep. Everything provided.'

'Is it awfully dear?'

'No. It seems this war bride outfit stakes out claims to these houses and then rents 'em on a pay-what-you-can basis.'

'We'd better jump at it,' said Sybil.

'That's what I think,' said Tim. He said

as much into the phone, then covered the mouthpiece again. 'We can have a look at the place this afternoon,' he told Sybil. 'And if we like it, we can move right in. Everything'll be ready. Seems there's a handyman who looks after the house and he'll have the lights and water turned on and a few supplies laid in.'

'Things are moving a little bit fast for me,' said Sybil, 'but I suppose we'd better do it. Ah, you Americans.'

'This is pretty darned fast even for, ah, us Americans,' said Tim. 'It's also pretty darned lucky. Shall I tell her okay?'

Sybil nodded. For a moment, Tim thought he saw a faint shadow of disappointment in her face, but it passed so quickly that he couldn't be sure. He told Mrs. Barrelforth okay.

'What's next on the agenda?' asked Sybil. 'Breakfast, I hope.'

'I knew there was something I wanted,' said Tim. 'Breakfast, by all means. I'll phone down.'

'And the afternoon papers,' said Sybil. 'I'm dying to read about the shooting.'

'The shooting?' repeated Tim vaguely.

Then he sat up straight in his chair beside the phone. 'Good God,' he exclaimed, 'I'd forgotten!'

'About the shooting?'

'Shooting, my eye. About you being Lady Sybil.'

'Oh,' said Sybil, 'that.' She wrinkled her nose. 'I wish you had forgotten that.'

'I'll try to,' said Tim. 'Otherwise, I won't dare kiss you without tugging at my forelock.'

'Let's see if you won't,' said Sybil.

★   ★   ★

Breakfast appeared, eventually, under gleaming dish covers among white napery, along with the newspapers, neatly folded. Sybil spread one out beside her on the sofa. 'Tim!' she exclaimed. 'Look.'

Tim was concentrating on tomato juice. 'Something about the shooting?' he asked.

'Something about it! It's in headlines a mile high. Red ones, too. Listen: Two die as gaming war flares. Socialites terrorized as mobsters invade Breeze Club.'

'Gosh,' said Tim. Then he chuckled. 'I suppose you'll always be convinced now that gangsters roam the city streets.'

'Don't they?'

'Man and boy, I never saw one. And you walk into a mob war your first night.'

'And loved it,' said Sybil. 'Shall I read you some more?'

'Go ahead,' said Tim. 'It sounds less sordid with your accent.'

'Sordid? With everybody in evening clothes? It was a very dressy affair.' She cleared her throat and read: 'Notables of the social and theatrical worlds scattered in panic early this morning when a band of gunmen forced their way into the notorious Breeze Club and staged a gun battle that left two of the participants dead on the red-carpeted floor.

'Police were convinced that the fray was connected with the efforts of Frank L. (Frankie) Heinkel, a big-time gambling operator of pre-war days, to obtain domination of the reviving underworld. Heinkel, whose career dates back to the Prohibition era, kept out of the public eye during the war, but there have been recent reports that he was trying to rebuild his organization.

'One of the slain men was identified as Louis Something-I-can't-pronounce, who was definitely linked by police to the Heinkel outfit. The other was Charles Something, a Breeze Club employee. The rest of the reputed Heinkel henchmen had made their escape by the time police reached the scene, and no arrests were made in connection with the actual shooting.

'However, police took into custody Jacob Burlick, manager of the Breeze Club — ' Sybil looked up. 'Why, that must be our friend Jake,' she said.

'No friend of mine,' said Tim.

' . . . and charged him,' Sybil read on, 'with operating an illicit gambling establishment. The club itself, which has long enjoyed a certain amount of immunity largely due to its inclusion of leading political figures among its patrons, was padlocked. Then,' she went on, 'there's a long list of all the important people who were on hand. Very impressive. No mention of us, though.'

45

'Just as well,' said Tim. 'Hardly the sort of thing an aspiring professor wants bandied about.'

'Mmm,' said Sybil. 'It would have been nice to send back to England.'

'Is there anything about What's-his-name? Magruder?'

'Not so far.' She ran her eye down the column. 'Oh,' she said suddenly.

'Find something?'

She didn't answer for a moment. Then she handed him the paper and pointed to a paragraph well down in the story. 'Read it yourself,' she said.

Tim read aloud: 'Police refused to confirm the report that a well-known figure in gambling circles was the target of the Heinkel invasion, nor would they answer questions speculating as to the identity of such a person. However, it was reliably learned that Samuel H. Magruder, so-called gentleman gambler of the pre-war days, slipped out of the Breeze Club just before the shooting started. Magruder, known among gamesters as Silky Sam, was never in the toils of the law, but he is definitely known to have had dealings with Heinkel before the war. There have also been reports of subsequent bad blood between them. An unidentified couple was said to have ducked out with Magruder.'

Sybil was silent. Tim noticed that her lips were trembling.

'Don't let it upset you, honey,' he said.

'I'm trying not to.'

He patted her hand. 'I know it must be a shock to learn that your father's supposed friend was a professional gambler.'

'Supposed friend?' Sybil's voice grew chilly. 'I shouldn't say so. Besides, he was a gentleman gambler. It says he was, right there in the paper.'

'How did your father make out with him? I believe you said they played bridge a good deal.'

'I've no idea. And it wouldn't have mattered to Father. He played because he loved the game. Furthermore, I want to see Mr. Magruder again.'

'All right,' said Tim. He didn't want Sybil to see his disapproval. 'You have his number, haven't you?'

'I seem to have lost it. I'm afraid it fell

out of my bag when I was chipping in on the cab fare home.'

'Maybe he's listed in the phone book.'

'No. I looked.'

'I mistrust people who aren't in phone books,' said Tim. 'Private phone numbers and foreign titles are considered very mistrustful in my provincial circles.' He grinned, but Sybil's answering smile was distraught.

'Tim,' she said, 'I wonder if our friend Jake would know how to reach him?'

'Must you keep referring to Jake as our friend?'

'He grows on me in retrospect. I wonder if the police would let us talk to him.'

'They might later on. I hardly think today would be the ideal time to ask.'

Sybil buttered a piece of toast. 'I suppose that's true,' she said.

'Besides,' added Tim, 'we ought to set out for this dream cottage pretty soon. I'd like to see it by daylight.'

'I'd make a little joke about a daydream cottage,' said Sybil, 'if I weren't so anxious about Mr. Magruder. Aside from everything else, we owe the dream cottage to him.'

'Do you really think so?'

'Don't you?'

'I don't know,' said Tim

'This war bride outfit sounds awfully respectable.'

'And you don't think my father's friends are respectable?'

'Well,' said Tim, 'his daughter was awfully forward for a lance corporal.'

'Don't try to mollify me,' said Sybil, looking mollified. 'Besides, how else could the war bride people have found out about us?'

5

Banshee Castle

It was after three when they finally set out for Merry Point. As they emerged from the Holland Tunnel onto the fog-bound Jersey flats, there hung already a desolate sense of approaching nightfall. Oncoming cars mostly had their lights on, yellow blobs bursting through the grayness, their wheels whirring shrilly on smooth wetness. Traffic moved swiftly, weaving, jockeying for advantage at stop signals, as though everyone wanted to get out of the cold fog and into warmth and cheer.

'Reminds me of Liverpool,' shivered Sybil.

'I have a feeling,' said Tim, 'that Liverpool will seem like the Riviera to you when we get to Merry Point.'

When they left the main highway and swung toward the coast, the sense of desolation deepened with the fading afternoon. Traffic thinned out, a relief at first, then dwindled to the point of loneliness. Roadside stands were shuttered, dine-and-dance places stood dark and gaunt. Signs advertising boating, bathing, and bungalows rattled in the wind. Occasionally they passed a shabby bar-and-grill or hamburger joint with its neon lights lit, but such forlorn bravado merely emphasized the general abandonment.

Even these relics of quasi-civilization petered out as they pushed south into the pine belt. Then the road ran somberly straight through endless tracts of pine trees, murmuring in their own funereal twilight. Mile after mile, the dark green wall rustled past. Once a lithe brown shape bounded across the road in front of them, and Tim said, 'Must remind you of the family deer park.'

'Was that really a deer?' asked Sybil.

'Sure.'

'Well, if my family ever had a deer park like this, I'm glad they didn't tell me about it.'

Suddenly the glow of lights appeared in

the distance and, almost before they knew it, they were coming into what according to the map must be Bankville, the town with the railroad station five miles from Merry Point. It was a relief to enter its bright main street after the brooding woodland. Behind lines of parked cars, shop windows were cheerful, light bulbs glittered around the marquee of a movie house, and potted shrubs lent wistful elegance to a little red-brick hotel.

'I suppose this'll be our shopping and whoopee center,' said Tim.

'We just passed a likely-looking pub,' said Sybil. 'I might add, why?'

'Because we probably wouldn't leave it,' said Tim.

'Who wants to leave it?' asked Sybil.

'Get thee behind me,' said Tim. But, having put the pub and the lights of Bankville behind him, he had to admit to himself that a spot of Dutch courage might have helped matters. Again the walls of pine closed in, fragrant and oppressive. It was decidedly dark by now, and the road that branched off to Merry Point was narrow and elusive in the mists swirling in front of the headlights. Among the trees, dark and shiny patches of water began to appear. Then, abruptly, the woodland ended, and the harsh salty smell of marsh and ocean rushed over them.

They emerged onto a flatland of stunted trees and waving reeds, palely illumined by a white and mist-hung moon just rising from a black expanse that had to be the Atlantic. On the sandspit that rose slightly from the marshland, rows of houses formed dim silhouettes like a village of cardboard.

'Darling,' said Sybil, 'let's go right straight back to that pub.'

'And let down your Mr. Magruder?'

'I'm sure Mr. Magruder had nothing to do with sending us to a place like this. This is the work of leprechauns.'

'I only hope a good, reliable leprechau has turned on the light and heat,' said Ti

'You mean we're going through with

'Don't you want to?'

'No,' said Sybil, 'but I suppose w to.'

They had reached the outskirt community, whose pattern lay a a wintry tree's in the moonlight. The road that had brought them across the marsh-land became the main street, parallel with the coast, and was lined with shuttered buildings, some of which appeared to be shops, tearooms, and such; while nearer the ocean, apparently fronting on the beach, rose the dark shapes of deserted houses. They were houses of an old-fashioned state-liness, with rambling porches crouched in shadows, and cupolas and turrets jutting weirdly against the pale sky.

'Try to imagine striped awnings,' said Tim, 'and children running around with buckets and shovels. Next thing is to ~ure out which of these is ours.'

~urs, all ours,' murmured Sybil. 'How ~ that would sound — to a couple ~es.'

~ed the car almost to a halt. 'The ~ said to keep straight through ~ come to a bridge. First ~ Sounds simple enough.' ~ must have it wrong.' ~h the empty street, ~o of silent houses. The ~cean grew loud in his ears. So, for that matter, was their breathing. A wooden bridge loomed out of the mist, crossing what seemed a sandy creek but which, seaward from the bridge, widened between gently rising bluffs until it met a phosphorescent surf licking at the sandbar guarding its mouth.

On the two tips of land above the sandbar's foam, there sat a pair of barnlike houses of the same general architecture as those they had passed. On the porch of the one on the far side of the inlet a yellow lamp burned.

'I guess that's the place,' said Tim. 'And judging from the light, our leprechaun's been there.'

'Darling,' said Sybil suddenly, 'I'm scared. I feel the way I did the night the buzz bomb missed us.'

Tim reached for her hand. 'If it turns out as well as that night did,' he said, 'I'll have no complaints.'

The car rattled across the loose planks of the bridge. Some fifty yards beyond, between two stone posts, a sandy drive curved away through rolling dunes toward the bluff. Tim swung the car into it. A quarter of a mile ahead of them, the big roof and chimneys of the house jutted above the dunes, dark-patched with catbriars and bayberry among the rippling beach grass.

The car crunched to a stop under an antique porte-cochere spreading from the porch whose ornate railings and columns curled around the brown-shingled walls of the house. The light they had seen came from an old lamp dangling on an iron chain in front of the entrance.

Below the house, the dunes dropped to a strip of beach that lay silvery in the misty light. A hundred yards from where they sat, the dim outline of a pier extended into dark water that churned into angry white around the pilings. Still further along, there thrust itself above the dunes a huge and fantastic openwork structure that looked like some gigantic toy left to rust on the sands. It took Tim several uneasy seconds to realize it was a Ferris wheel.

From somewhere in the direction of the pier came a scream.

'What's that?' cried Sybil, seizing Tim's arm.

It came again, raucous and shrill. A

moment later, a great bird rose from the dunes and sailed across the beach.

'Seagull,' said Tim.

'More like a vulture,' said Sybil.

'A nice, cheerful thought with which to enter our connubial bower,' said Tim. 'Shall I carry you across the threshold?'

'Maybe you'd better. My knees are shaking.'

'I'm willing to try,' said Tim. He jumped out of the car, went round to the other side, and lifted her from the seat.

'I'm a pretty big girl,' said Sybil.

'Light as a feather,' said Tim. 'A vulture feather.'

He carried her up the steps to the porch, trying not to wheeze audibly. At the front door, embedded in a border of stained glass, he paused. 'Look,' he said. 'There's a note.'

'I know what it says,' murmured Sybil. ' "Don't enter this house if you value your life.' And underneath is a crudely drawn skull.'

'At least it's in pencil and not in blood,' said Tim. He set Sybil on her feet and reached for the paper with an assurance he didn't feel. He read it aloud: 'Mr. Ludlow. I been over today and got the burner going and the water and lights turned on. Also brung up some wood for the fireplace there is plenty more in the cellar. Left you some beer and cans of beans and stuff in the icebox in case you need same. Key is under the mat. Hope everything is satisfactory. Yours truly, Elias Whittlebait.'

Tim found the key under the mat, opened the door, and carried Sybil into the house's warmth. He kissed her again, put her down, and felt for the light switch. They were standing in a broad hallway from which rose a majestic, if slightly sagging, staircase. The woodwork was dark, and there was a rather frightening hat-stand with intricately carved serpents twining around a long mirror.

To their right, through green portieres, a doorway opened into a big, comfortable-looking living room. It was papered in a deep yellow that bore signs of a long-faded pattern. Green curtains hung at its many windows. The furniture was a hodge-podge of solid old pieces and flimsy summery items. There were a couple of black leather easy chairs, a black leather davenport, and an oak table with a green glass-shaded lamp on it. There were also a number of wicker chairs and a wicker settee, all heaped with cushions that once must have been bright but were now a genteel neutral.

The cheeriest feature of the room was a great brick fireplace with a log fire neatly laid. Above it hung a seascape in oil, framed in gilt, and on the opposite wall a stuffed tarpon was mounted on a board with printed data regarding its demise, also in gilt.

Beyond the living room, through French doors, was a library, considerably smaller and lined with glass-doored bookcases. It contained a roll-top desk.

Across the hallway was the dining room with big curtained windows and paintings of dead fish and rabbits and ducks that looked down on a heavy oval table and chairs of oak.

'Darling,' said Sybil, looking around, 'I've been a goose. It's lovely. I knew Mr. Magruder would take care of us.'

'Mr. Magruder and his leprechauns,'

said Tim. 'I admit it's better than anything I expected. Shall we explore upstairs?'

'I'd like to explore a bathroom,' said Sybil. She glanced toward the staircase, from the head of which came the faint sound of windows rattling in the wind. 'Wonder if there's one on this floor,' she added with a sheepish grin. 'I'm not quite ready to go poking upstairs.'

Tim tried a door under the staircase. 'Here's a lavatory,' he said. 'I'll bring in the bags.'

It took him several trips to bring in all of Sybil's trim airplane luggage and his own collection of suitcases and duffel bags, which he piled in the hallway. Sybil emerged from the lavatory and said, 'The w.c. doesn't flush.'

'We'll put the leprechaun on it tomorrow,' said Tim.

'How would that help?'

'I mean on the job of fixing it.'

'Oh,' said Sybil. 'I wondered. What was his name again?'

'Elias Whittlebait.'

'Lovely name. Must be a lovely little

man. And how about a lovely little dry martini before we unpack?'

'Fine. Let's see, one of these duffel bags has the drinkables in it.' He found the right bag and carried it into the kitchen.

Sybil, following, gave a little cry of pleasure at its shiny whiteness. 'What beautiful things I'll cook here,' she exclaimed. 'Beginning with the martinis. You light the fire while I mix 'em.'

Tim went back to the living room and knelt in front of the fireplace. He touched a match to the wadded paper under the logs and watched with enjoyment as tiny shoots of flame burst upward, gathering momentum until the fireplace was full of crackling light.

'Tim!' He heard Sybil's voice across the hall, sharp and taut. '*Tim!*'

He turned on his haunches to see her coming toward him from the dining room. Her face was white. 'There's someone moving around on the porch,' she said.

'Must be the wind.'

'No,' said Sybil. 'Look!' She pointed

61

toward the dining room window. Unmistakably, against its dark pane, was pressed a man's face.

'Probably Elias Whittlebait having a look around,' said Tim. Even to him, the words sounded hollow.

'Why wouldn't he come to the front door?'

'I'll soon find out.' He started toward the door.

'Wait,' said Sybil. 'Take this.' She picked up the poker from its rack by the fireplace and thrust it at him.

'What would I do with that?' asked Tim.

'I don't know,' said Sybil, 'but it'll make me feel better.'

'All right,' said Tim, trying to smile. He took the poker and went to the front door. The wind thudded against it as he turned the knob, as if it had been waiting for a long time to get in. The comfortable solidity of the house dissolved suddenly into the eerie loneliness that had hung over it when they arrived. Tim gripped the poker and pushed the door open.

'Who's there?' he called.

For a moment, there was only the rush of the wind and the roar of the surf. Then a thickset figure emerged from the shadows along the porch and, in the thin glow of the lamp overhead, Tim saw a pistol pointed at him.

6

No Fourth for Bridge

'Better drop that poker,' said the man with the pistol.

Tim thought he better had, too, but he also thought he should show some gumption. 'Why?' he asked.

'Because I have you covered with a thirty-two automatic, son, and I'm in a position to give orders.' The man's voice was gruff and businesslike, but not unfriendly. Tim could see him more clearly now. He appeared to be past middle age and he was wearing a buttoned-up windbreaker and a soft hat.

'Guess you're right,' said Tim, and let the poker fall.

'That's better,' said the man. 'Suppose you tell me just what you're doing here?'

'I'm living here,' said Tim.

The man's eyes seemed to be gauging him for a moment; then, as if he'd reached a decision, he put the automatic into his

64

pocket. 'If you live here, son,' he said, 'then I'm probably trespassing. Are you the veteran with the English bride?'

'Yep.'

'In that case, I owe you an apology. Never dreamed you'd get here so quick.' He stepped forward and thrust out his hand. 'My name is Squareless. John Squareless. I live across the inlet.'

'Glad to meet you,' said Tim, shaking hands.

'I saw your lights and thought something funny was going on. Didn't expect you for another week. So I rowed over for a look. Quicker than walking around by the bridge and better exercise. Well, sorry to have disturbed you.'

'Don't mention it,' said Tim. 'Won't you come in?'

Squareless hesitated. Tim got the curious impression that he wanted to come in very much but that something was holding him back. Just then Sybil appeared in the doorway's square of light. 'Hello,' she said, 'what's up?'

'Turns out to be a neighborly call,' said Tim. 'This is Mr. Squareless, from across the way.'

'Delighted,' said Sybil.

'Pleased to meet you,' said Squareless. He was staring hard at Sybil, so hard that it became embarrassing, as he finally seemed to realize. 'Excuse me,' he said. 'I couldn't help thinking for a moment that I'd met you before.'

'It's not impossible. I've knocked around.'

'So've I,' said Squareless. 'But I was mistaken — '

'Do come in,' said Sybil. 'I was just mixing a cocktail.'

'You're very kind,' said Squareless. Again he hesitated, and again he seemed to reach a decision. 'All right. For a minute.'

He walked into the hall and hung his hat and windbreaker on the serpentine coat-stand. Tim saw that he was a man of perhaps sixty, built so solidly as to seem shorter than his five feet nine or ten, but with an easy grace to his movements. He had a rounded outdoors face with a blunt nose, and a mouth that was slow to smile but smiled thoroughly when it did. His hair was sparse and grizzled. It struck Tim that he bore a resemblance to Winston Churchill.

66

'Take a seat by the fire, Mr. Squareless,' said Sybil. 'I'll fetch the martinis.'

Squareless lowered himself into one of the black leather chairs and looked around the room. 'Place hasn't changed much,' he said. 'First time I've been inside it in more than twenty years.'

'Really?' said Tim.

Squareless nodded broodingly. 'Twenty-four years, to be exact.' He reached in the pocket of his tweed coat and brought out a pipe and tobacco pouch. 'Think your wife'll mind if I smoke this?'

'I think we can risk it,' said Tim. He waited a moment, but Squareless was silent. 'I don't mean to pry, sir,' said Tim, 'but I'm a bit curious about this house to begin with, and I can't help wondering why you should have boycotted its owner for twenty-four years.'

'Its owner?' repeated Squareless. 'I'm its owner.'

Sybil had just entered the room with an amber pitcher and three glasses on a tray. 'What!' she exclaimed. 'You're our landlord?'

'I'm not quite sure what my status is,' said Squareless. 'You see, I was approached by this British-American War Brides Association outfit, which was getting together a list of available houses, particularly along the coast where a lot of furnished houses stand empty all winter. Most of 'em, of course, don't have any heating, but even the few that do aren't in much demand. Too godforsaken for most people.'

'Quite,' murmured Sybil.

'Anyway,' went on Squareless, accepting a martini, 'this bunch of old gals, who I understand were war brides themselves years ago, bulldozed a lot of sentimental old duffers like me into turning our houses over to 'em. Seemed sensible enough, and it's been no trouble. The gals even arranged for a handyman to look after the place. They take care of the rent, too. Which leaves me a landlord in name only.'

'Good,' said Sybil. 'If you don't mention the rent, I won't mention the w.c. that doesn't flush.'

'Agreed,' said Squareless.

'I suppose you let this house in summer, normally,' said Tim.

Squareless nodded, puffing on his pipe. 'Both these houses have been in my family for a good many years,' he said. 'But if you don't mind, I'd rather not talk about it. This house has some unhappy memories for me. Let's let it go at that.'

There was a moment of strained silence, then Sybil asked, 'Were the arrangements — the arrangements for us coming here, I mean — made by a Mrs. Barrelforth?'

'Some such name,' said Squareless. 'It was all done by correspondence. Whoever it was didn't bother to tell me when to expect you.'

'Somebody expected us,' said Tim. 'A Mr. Whittlebait.'

'Who?' said Squareless. 'Oh, you mean the handyman. I suppose the old gals got into touch with him directly.'

'He must be a very good handyman,' said Sybil. 'He had the house in apple-pie order.'

'Don't think I know him,' said Squareless. 'The fellow who looks after it in summer has gouged enough out of me to treat himself to Florida this winter. This Whittlebait's probably a cousin or something. They're all related to each other, these Pinies.'

69

'Pinies?' said Sybil.

'I keep forgetting you're new arrivals,' said Squareless. 'That's the somewhat slighting name attached to a perfectly worthy group of citizens who live back in the pine woods out of reach of hurricanes, tidal waves, and other phenomena of the ocean-front. They make a living mostly off the summer people, whose lawns they mow and whose hedges they clip. They're a self-contained little bunch and they're suspicious of reading and writing, but they're perfectly honest and well-behaved.'

'We don't have to worry about arrows quivering in the front door?' asked Sybil.

'Sorry, but the Pinies aren't likely to provide you with any excitement.'

'But, Mr. Squareless,' said Sybil, 'you must have thought somebody was capable of providing some excitement hereabouts tonight.'

Squareless looked at her from under his shaggy eyebrows. 'True,' he said. 'But I wasn't thinking of Pinies. I was thinking of ghosts.'

Tim and Sybil both jumped. Squareless

smiled and took his pipe out of his mouth. 'There was a time,' he said, 'when this wasn't quite the peaceful little resort it now appears. During the sorry days of Prohibition, this little inlet was highly favored by the rum-running gentry for obvious reasons. For a while, in fact, this area was a headquarters for some very fancy operators. So when I speak of ghosts, I do so as they speak of Captain Kidd's ghost in the West Indies.'

'You mean these people went on using the place after Repeal?' asked Tim.

'They tried to. I suppose they'd learned to like the ocean air. At any rate, they went on running a casino, and for a few years they had quite an establishment. In fact, that's why this side of the inlet, as you may have noticed, has gone downhill, at least from the point of view of the other side. An amusement pier was built, and all sorts of claptrap concessions were strung along the boardwalk, and cheap boarding-houses went up — all designed to attract what the other side considers an undesirable element. I personally consider all summer people undesirable, but

I can see how the solid burghers of the one side were a little upset by the various skin-game operators and gamblers and occasional gangsters that moved in on the other.'

'Is that why you live on the respectable side?' asked Sybil.

'Not entirely,' said Squareless.

'I only wondered,' said Sybil, 'if you disapproved of gambling.'

'Well, no,' said Squareless, 'not in general. I disapprove of the sort of gambling that went on in that casino, which, I am happy to add, burned down some time before the war. But I've done a good deal of friendly gambling in my day.'

'What I am leading up to,' said Sybil, 'is, do you play bridge?'

'I used to play a great deal of bridge,' replied Squareless. 'Rather good at it, too. But I haven't played much since — since I became a recluse.' He smiled. 'You can't be a recluse and play bridge.'

'But wouldn't you play with us?' pleaded Sybil. 'If we could find a fourth?'

'A fourth?' said Squareless. 'Ay, there's the rub.'

'As distinct from the rubber,' said Tim.

'Oh, there must be a fourth around somewhere,' said Sybil impatiently. 'After all, this isn't the Fiji Islands.'

'It might as well be,' said Squareless.

'I can't believe it.'

'After all, dear,' said Tim, 'if Mr. Squareless, who has lived here all his life, doesn't know of a fourth, you're hardly likely to dig one up in a couple of days.'

'We'll see,' said Sybil.

'I haven't exactly lived here all my life,' said Squareless. 'Please don't think me that provincial. In my younger days, I did a good bit of wandering around the world. Enjoyed it, too. It's only lately that I decided I wanted peace more than anything else and came back here to find it. There's plenty of it here. Too much for most people.'

'Do you live alone?' asked Sybil curiously.

Squareless looked at her before he answered. Then he said, 'With a house-keeper. And she doesn't play bridge.' He emptied his glass and rose abruptly. 'This has been very pleasant,' he said. 'I hope you have an enjoyable winter. In spite of ghosts.'

He started toward the door. Sybil followed him.

'If we could find a fourth,' she began, 'would you — '

'I don't know,' said Squareless. He reached for his hat and windbreaker, then turned on her almost fiercely. 'I don't know, I tell you,' he snapped. 'Stop asking questions.'

Then he walked quickly into the darkness.

7

Husband Copes with Prowlers

Sometime during the night, Tim was awakened by Sybil shaking his shoulder. She was sitting up in bed. 'Tim,' she was saying, 'Tim, there's somebody down on the beach.'

'Huh, whuzzit?'

'I saw a light on the beach.'

Tim sat up sleepily beside her and focused his eyes on the window. It was a big window, and the moonlight, fading and brightening as patches of cloud streamed across the sky, filled the bedroom that Mr. Whittlebait had apparently chosen for them. At least, he had made up the four-poster bed across which the pale light was now drifting.

'Don' see anything,' said Tim.

'It was there a second ago. It just went out.'

Tim's eyes began to function more

normally. He could see the shadowy dunes now, and beyond them the gleaming beach and the long outline of the pier.

'Probably a blob of phosphorus in the water,' he said.

'Look,' said Sybil. 'Is that phosphorus?'

A tiny circle of light appeared suddenly near the foot of the pier, then vanished again.

'Well, no,' said Tim.

'Well then?'

Tim sighed. He was wide awake now. 'I have a feeling,' he said, 'that we're embarking on an old traditional bedroom scene. Wife hears burglar downstairs. Husband says it's termites. Wife says all right, if that's the kind of man he is, she'll go downstairs and cope with the burglar single-handed.'

'He doesn't let her do it, does he?'

'He does if they've been married long enough,' said Tim.

'Have we?'

'Almost. What time is it?'

Sybil stretched for her watch on the bedside table. 'Half-past two.'

Tim scratched his tousled head and

grinned at her. 'Do you really want me to have a look?'

'I'm afraid so. Do you mind awfully?'

'I guess not.'

'Think how nice and cozy it will be when you get back.'

'Look,' said Tim, 'that's the principle of beating your head on the wall, because it feels so good when you stop. However . . .' He sighed and climbed out of bed, growling at the cold floor. He found his shoes and put them on.

'Take the poker,' said Sybil.

'It doesn't help. People just tell me to put it down and I do. Leaves me at a disadvantage.'

'Haven't we any firearms of any sort? No war trophies?'

'By George,' said Tim, 'I do have a Luger, at that. It's somewhere in the luggage. Unloaded, though.'

'I wish you'd take it with you, even so.'

'I'll see if I can find it.'

He clattered downstairs, his shoes flopping loosely without socks. Most of the luggage was still in the hall, and he undid a duffel bag and fumbled through it until he found the Luger. He found a flashlight, too. Then he took his weather-stained trenchcoat from the stand, slipped it over his pajamas, and put the Luger and the flashlight in the pockets. He felt vaguely foolish, the way he had some-times felt when his jeep roared into a freshly captured town and deposited him in battle dress at the local museum.

It had turned into a comparatively pleasant night. The wind had shifted and felt almost balmy as it flapped the trenchcoat around his legs. The moon was momentarily obscured by a mass of clouds, but enough light seeped through to envelop the dunes in a ghostly pallor. Tim slogged through them, sinking and sliding in the sand, which rapidly filled his shoes.

The Atlantic had quieted to a rhythmic purr, a silky sound above which, sud-denly, Tim was sure he heard the splash of oars. Somebody else thought so, too, because the little circle of light appeared again, this time near the end of the pier, and its beam swung across the dark water. Then, with the unreality of a slick stage effect, it picked out the bobbing shape of a rowboat with a huddled figure in it. Instantly the light went out.

Tim stood still in the shelter of the dunes. The foot of the pier, which as far as he could tell in the dimness was reached by some sort of stairs, was about twenty-five yards away. It seemed to converge with a boardwalk that extended, flat and nebulous, along the shoreline in the opposite direction. The pier itself was cluttered with indefinable structures that blocked the view.

Then, softly hollow, Tim heard footsteps coming toward him over the planking of the pier. They were coming fast but not running. Then they slowed, and two figures emerged cautiously from between two buildings near the entrance to the pier. They paused and seemed to be whispering together. It looked to Tim as if they had been rattled by the apparition of the rowboat, and he decided that it might be a good idea to rattle them some more before they recovered.

He put on his sternest classroom voice. 'What's going on?' he called.

'Mother of God,' cried one of the figures aloud. It wasn't a curse, either. It sounded, rather, like a man who was used to cursing and had to put special appeal in his voice when he wanted it to count.

Simultaneously the other figure sent the beam of the flashlight in Tim's direction. Tim dropped behind the dune and closed his fingers on the Luger's butt. 'Come, come,' he called, 'speak up.' It occurred to him immediately afterward that this phrase smacked all too much of the classroom.

The man with the flashlight spoke. 'Take it easy, mac,' he said. 'Don't get excited.'

'I'm not excited,' said Tim. 'Just curious.'

'Wise guy, eh?' This came from the first figure, who had evidently been reassured by Tim's attempt to sound tough. The other man shushed him.

'Okay, mac,' he said. 'We been fishin', that's all.'

'At this time of night?' asked Tim.

'Hell, yes. It's the best time.'

This, for all Tim knew, was true.

80

Whether it was or not, he didn't see what he could do about it. The pier, presumably, was public. No riparian rights seemed to be involved. As a man whose only immediate interest was to go back to bed, he felt he had done his duty.

'Okay,' he said. 'Skip it.'

'Okay,' said the man with the flashlight.

'Wait a minute,' said the other man. 'Who the hell are you, anyway?'

'Shut up, you damned fool,' said the other. 'So long, mac.'

'So long,' said Tim. He felt more than ever as he had when his conquering hero's entry wound up among the Etruscan vases.

The flashlight was doused, and the two men sauntered down the boardwalk with what struck Tim as elaborate carelessness. As far as he was aware, though, nobody was ever hanged for elaborate carelessness.

He waited, crouched among the dunes, until the two figures had melted into the darkness. A minute or so later, as he turned back toward the house, he heard the sound of an automobile starting.

At the front porch, he sat and emptied the sand out of his shoes. He carried them into the house and upstairs.

Sybil, in her blue pajamas, sat on the edge of the bed. 'I was watching through the window,' she said. 'What was it all about?'

'Damned if I know,' said Tim. 'Couple of guys said they'd been fishing. Maybe they had.'

'Did they have any fish?'

'Not that I noticed. But that wouldn't prove they weren't fishing.'

'Were they the sporting type?'

'I'm no judge of the sporting type.'

'A pity,' said Sybil. 'Maybe I should have gone after all.'

'They'd certainly have taken you for the sporting type if you had.'

Sybil snuggled warm against him. 'In a ladylike way,' she said, 'I am.'

8

Cold-Blooded Peeping Tom

Sunshine poured in through the big window, bathing the four-poster in brightness and warmth. Sybil sat up and stretched and cried, 'Oh, darling, what a wonderful morning!'

'Looks all right from here,' said Tim.

Sybil jumped out of bed and leaned across the window sill. 'It looks all right from everywhere. The ocean is positively dancing. Can't be the same one as last night.'

It was certainly a gorgeous expanse of blue that lay outside the window. Little breakers tumbled out of its edges and chased each other up the white beach. The land, too, seemed almost to glisten in the golden October haze. The dunes were rolling patterns of dark greens and russets against silver. Even the deserted pier, the boardwalk, and the Ferris wheel caught the sparkle. Everything that had seemed ominous and strange the night before was now all smiles and innocence.

'Listen to the gulls,' said Sybil, pointing to half a dozen or so that were wheeling above the water's edge. 'They sound like choirboys.'

The only somber note on the horizon was the tall brown house on the opposite point, with half its windows shuttered.

'Darling,' said Sybil, twisting toward him, 'know what I think I'll do?'

'Sleep for another couple of hours,' yawned Tim.

'No.'

'Cook an enormous breakfast?'

'Later on, maybe. But first.'

'Take a bath?'

'Yes. But where?'

Tim sat up suddenly among the covers. 'My God,' he said, 'you don't mean in the ocean?'

'I certainly do. We used to swim much later than this in Cornwall.'

'This isn't Cornwall. The Gulf Stream —'

'I know all about the Gulf Stream.'

'You haven't a bathing suit.'

84

'What of it?' She strolled toward the bathroom, unbuttoning her pale blue pajama coat. A moment later she came back with a fluffy white towel draped around her. 'You won't join me?'

'No, thanks. Somebody's got to stay ashore and handle the crowds.'

'Piffle. There's no one around.'

'Mr. Squareless, for a start.'

'It would brighten his gray life,' said Sybil. 'Anyway, he can't see around the point. I'll go in on the far side, by the pier.'

'If you start to freeze,' said Tim, 'don't expect me to swim out with a bottle of brandy around my neck.'

'Most men would be glad to,' said Sybil. She blew him a kiss and went out.

Tim listened to her bare feet on the stairs, then he got out of bed and stood by the window. Sybil appeared from under the porte-cochere and picked her way daintily across the dunes, her long legs, under the sketchy white cloak, moving with graceful sureness. She reached the beach and, tossing the towel aside, turned to wave, a moment's tableau against the clean white and blue. Then she ran lightly across the sand toward the shifting lace of the surf.

Watching her, Tim felt again as he had when they first arrived in their hotel room, as if he had been thrown into the company of a lovely, wanton stranger. Then he gave a chuckle as she dipped a toe into the water's curving edge and turned back. That was no lovely, wanton stranger. That was his wife.

She scurried back to the dunes and picked up the towel, then headed for the house, running and slipping through the sand. Tim watched her for a moment, then put on his bathrobe and slippers and went downstairs to meet her at the door.

'Don't stand there beaming I-told-you-so,' snapped Sybil before he could speak. 'I came back because there's a peeping Tom on the pier.'

'No jury would convict,' said Tim.

Sybil glanced with modest satisfaction at her ill-clothed two thirds. 'The trouble is,' she said, 'that he didn't really peep. He didn't whistle or leer or anything. He didn't even look interested.'

'Must have been asleep.'

'His eyes were open. I think he was something else.'

'Drunk?'

'Dead.'

Tim looked dubious. 'Last night it was screams, death notes, and burglars,' he said. 'Today it's a corpse.'

'I can't help it. I want you to look at him.'

'Okay, but it's going to be embarrassing if he's not dead. What'll I do? Ask him how he dares sit on a public pier while my wife September-morns?'

'Ask him how he dares not to look interested,' said Sybil. 'Anyway, the pier's supposed to be closed. Come on.'

'Not with you in a towel.'

Sybil made a face at him and took a rough tweed coat from the stand and buttoned it around her.

Tim said, 'That's better. Now I can concentrate.'

They walked across the dunes in the crisp sunlight. Tim paused to kick off his slippers, which he stuck in his bathrobe pockets, and the warm sand felt good between his toes. The whole morning felt good, for that matter, and he couldn't seriously believe anything was amiss. He even began to whistle as they neared the foot of the pier, which, Tim saw, joined the end of the boardwalk at right angles.

Ramshackle wooden steps led up to it from the beach and a red and yellow sign beside them said: No Dogs or Bicycles on Boardwalk. The vague structures Tim had noticed on the pier the night before proved now to be a haphazard collection of small shuttered buildings, in need of paint but still boasting their summer glory in faded letters: The Nik-Nak Shop, Pantry Luncheonette, Sportland, Everybody Wins a Prize. Between them extended a wooden bar with a piece of cardboard nailed to it that stated: Pier Closed. Keep Off.

'You see,' said Sybil, 'he had no business being there.'

'Neither do we,' said Tim. 'And neither did those guys last night.'

'Good lord,' exclaimed Sybil, 'I'd quite forgotten about them. Maybe they killed him. Hurry!'

Tim followed her up the steps with a

skeptical grin; but after they ducked under the barrier, he felt his confidence ebbing. There was an uncanny desolation about the empty buildings, as if they had been left like this in the wake of a plague. Even the garish gaiety of their signs had a chilling quality, suggesting that witches held their midnight sabbats here, screaming 'Bingo!' in shrill cackles.

Tim and Sybil padded along the pier, its boards pleasantly sun-warmed under their bare feet. It ended in a sort of square veranda evidently designed for those who didn't want to play bingo, simplified or otherwise, but only to sit in the sunlight. Around three sides of it ran a continuous bench, its back formed by the railings of the pier.

On the northern side, facing the inlet, sat a man. His body was slumped sideways and slightly twisted so that his head was turned three quarters toward the sea, his chin resting on the railing and an arm hanging limp on either side. From the beach he might have appeared to be a comfortably sprawled lounger, but from where Tim and Sybil stood, a grotesque rigidity in the limbs left no room for doubt.

'You were right this time,' Tim said with grim apology. He glanced at her and saw that her face was sickly white. 'You stay here. I'll have a look at him.'

He approached the body, unconsciously tiptoeing for no good reason. It was clad in workmen's clothes, blue denim trousers, an old brown coat out at the elbows, and a cheap lumberjack shirt. A slouch hat was pulled hall over the face, and from under its brim a trickle of blood had left its crusty path, staining the light gray stubble of one cheek.

'Don't touch him,' called Sybil nervously.

'Won't hurt to see what hit him,' said Tim. Gingerly he took the hat brim between thumb and forefinger and raised it a little. Near the right temple was a little round hole, the flesh around it burned reddish-brown.

Behind him, suddenly, Sybil gave a little scream. He turned to see her with her hand pressed against her mouth, her eyes wide and horrified.

'Don't let it upset you, dear,' said Tim anxiously. He lowered the hat brim as he had found it and hurried to her. 'That's no way for an old lance corporal to act,' he added with what was meant to be soothing jocularity.

'Sorry,' said Sybil. 'Sorry.' She choked on the words and blinked hard, as if trying to get control of herself. In a moment, she managed to speak more calmly. 'Probably suicide, don't you think?'

'I don't think so,' said Tim.

'Why not? He could have sat there, taken a last look at the ocean and then shot himself. His head would have fallen the way it is now, wouldn't it? And his arm would have dropped outside the railing the way it is, and the gun gone into the water.'

'True enough,' said Tim. 'Also, somebody might have arranged him that way. A couple of somebodies whom a certain husband, at the behest of his wife, had a few words with last night.'

'Oh, dear,' cried Sybil worriedly. 'I should never have let you go.'

'So I thought at the time,' said Tim. He

smiled and patted her arm.

'You're only guessing it's not suicide, aren't you?' she asked.

'No,' said Tim, 'I'm not guessing. There's no bullet hole in the hat.'

'Oh,' said Sybil. She was silent for a while, leaning against his shoulder. Then she asked, 'I suppose we should notify the police?'

'Yes.'

She hesitated. 'There's no need to tell them about last night, is there?'

'About the men on the pier? I think I should.'

'Why? Why should you get mixed up in it?'

'I won't get mixed up.'

'Of course you will, if you tell them. You'll have to be a witness at all sorts of proceedings and you'll be asked to identify suspects and heaven knows what all. You'll have precious little time for any Ph.D.s.'

'It's a matter of civic duty,' said Tim.

'It will probably be strongly implied,' said Sybil, 'that you failed in your civic duty by letting the men get away.'

'By God,' said Tim, 'if they start anything like that — '

'See? You'll simply be making trouble for yourself if you mention it.'

Tim glanced at her curiously. 'You seem unduly anxious to have me forget about it.'

'Of course I am,' said Sybil. 'For the reasons I've just stated.' She spread her hands a little, as if to say 'Q.E.D.'

Tim continued to stare. 'You know,' he said slowly, 'I have a foolish sort of notion that I've seen that chap before someplace. Do you have it, too?'

'No.'

'Hallucination, probably,' said Tim. 'Let's get back to the house.'

9

Whittlebait is a Modest Man

Walking up through the dunes, Sybil said, 'It must be one of those people Mr. Squareless was telling us about. What was the word? Pinies.'

'My God,' said Tim. 'I hope it isn't Mr. Whittlebait.'

'Goodness, what a selfish remark. Besides, who would want to kill our poor leprechaun?'

'Somebody who envied him his chance to be near you. Especially since you've taken to running around with no clothes on.'

Sybil sighed. 'I can remember when you liked me with no clothes on.'

Tim said, 'I'm wondering if we have a telephone to call the police.'

'You're not going to tell them about last night, are you?' Sybil asked.

'I don't know. Haven't made up my mind.'

'If you do,' said Sybil, 'the honeymoon really will be over.'

They had emerged from the dunes and were crossing the gravel driveway to the porte-cochere under which Tim's car was still standing. Hard to realize, he thought, that it wasn't much more than twelve hours since he had left it there. They mounted the porch stairs and went into the house, which looked bright and cheerful in the morning sun.

'Seems to me I saw a phone in the library,' said Tim. He went into the living-room and through the French doors. 'Here we are,' he called. Then, a moment later, he called again. 'It's dead, damn it.'

'Dead!' cried Sybil from the hallway. 'Who?'

'The phone, dear, only the phone,' said Tim, coming back to the hall. 'We'll have to get it connected. Meanwhile, we'd better drive to Bankville. I suppose that's the nearest police station. Although we might see if our neighbor, Squareless, has a phone.'

'He said he was a recluse. Recluses

95

don't have phones.'

'A really serious recluse likes to have a phone so he can let it ring,' said Tim. 'However, I guess it would be better, at that, if we went straight to the police.'

'You go, darling,' said Sybil. 'I'll stay here.'

Tim looked surprised. 'I didn't think you'd want to be left alone after — after what's happened.'

'I've recovered now,' said Sybil. 'Besides, it'll take me ages to dress, and I can be getting breakfast ready.'

'Make it a big one,' said Tim. 'It may sound ghoulish, but the morning's activity has given me a whale of an appetite.'

He went upstairs and pulled a sweater and a pair of pants over his pajamas, stuck his feet into sneakers, and came back down. At the doorway Sybil said, 'Darling, I'm quite serious about not telling the police any more than you have to.'

'It probably would mean a lot of fuss and feathers,' admitted Tim.

'So you won't?'

'All right,' said Tim. 'It's a promise.'

'Seal it.'

He sealed it so thoroughly that when he finally released her, he couldn't remember for a minute what he was supposed to be doing.

★　★　★

She stood on the porch waving to him until the old sedan disappeared among the green-gray dunes. It reappeared on the little white bridge across the inlet and she waved again. Then it was gone. Sybil waited a moment or so, biting her lip thoughtfully. Then she thrust her hands deep into the pockets of the tweed coat and with an expression of tight determination she headed for the beach.

When she reached the last dune, she paused and looked around. There was no living thing in sight except a solemn conclave of seagulls standing on the sand. The bluff on which the house stood hid her from the Squareless mansion, although it was apparent that the end of the pier, jutting well beyond the point of land, was visible from their neighbor's windows. Well, she thought, she'd have to risk that.

She pattered up the steps to the board-walk and slipped across it to the pier, then moved cautiously from building to building. As she neared the square veranda at the pier's end, she felt her breath coming faster. The unpleasant thought occurred to her that the killer or killers might return to the scene; might even then be somewhere among the silent, shuttered buildings.

The veranda, in the sunlight, was unchanged. The shabbily clad figure was still slumped across the bench. Once again, Sybil looked in every direction. Then, with the twisted face of a car-sick child trying not to throw up, she crept across the warm planking to the body and knelt beside it. Swiftly her hands went through the pockets of the threadbare coat.

Somewhere behind her a board creaked. She froze into terrified immobility, as motionless as the waxen thing beside her. Seconds of silence went by, silence broken only by the water lapping at the pilings under her. She went through the pockets of the denim trousers.

Finally she stood up, her face weary

and frustrated and green. Nausea suddenly gripped her throat and she barely made the railing before she was actively sick.

Grimly she forced herself to turn once again to the dead man. Carefully, even artistically, she adjusted the slouch hat until it looked as if it had been idly shoved to the back of his head by the wearer. The bullet hole stared, like a hideous third eye, from beneath the brim.

Sybil stepped back and considered her handiwork with a mixture of revulsion and satisfaction. Then she turned and ran along the pier.

She was weak and shaky when she got back to the house. As she entered the hall, she heard a door slam from the direction of the kitchen and jumped like a frightened rabbit. She steadied herself on the newel post and called in a loud and artificial voice, 'Who's there?'

Nobody answered, but she was sure she heard someone moving in the kitchen. 'Who's there?' she cried again, this time with a suggestion of panic.

The swinging door from the kitchen

opened and a mild face peered around it into the dining room. 'It's only me, ma'am,' said a meek, nasal voice. 'Elias Whittlebait.'

'Oh,' said Sybil. She clung to the newel post and laughed, almost hysterically.

Elias Whittlebait looked hurt. He was a smallish man, pale and thin, with a walrus mustache that seemed too big for his face. His eyes were blue and, behind thick-lensed spectacles, looked watery. He was wearing blue denim overalls and a coat to match, a collarless shirt, and a cap.

He took the cap off and said, 'Are you all right, ma'am?' The uneasy question might have referred to her mental condition.

'Yes,' gasped Sybil, struggling to control the intensity of her relief. 'Yes, Mr. Whittlebait, I'm quite all right. I thought you were a burglar.'

'No burglars around these parts,' said Mr. Whittlebait with a reassuring smile. 'Even if there was, you wouldn't have to worry with me lookin' after the place.'

'I'm quite sure we wouldn't, Mr. Whittlebait.' She had been trying to think what he reminded her of and she remembered now: Bill the Lizard, of Wonderland.

'Thank you, ma'am,' said Mr. Whittlebait modestly. 'I come round to see if everything was satisfactory.'

'Everything's splendid, thanks.'

'Glad to hear it,' said Mr. Whittlebait. 'Particularly you bein' a stranger to our shores and your husband one of the boys that fought to preserve our way of life.' The little speech sounded as if he had practiced it.

'That's very nice,' said Sybil.

'So, if there's anything I can do to make you comfortable — '

Sybil hesitated, then decided not to mention the corpse on the pier. Tim would be contacting the police. Instead, she said: 'Oh, yes, there is. The w.c. on this floor doesn't work.'

'The what, ma'am?'

'Of course, you don't call it that in this country, do you? The bathroom. The toilet.'

Mr. Whittlebait averted his eyes. 'Oh,' he said, 'you mean the commode. You mean it don't — flush.'

'That's it.'

'I'll take a look.' He went into the lavatory under the stairs, and she could hear clanking noises. Presently he came out, still looking embarrassed. 'I'll have to get some tools for that,' he said. 'I'll be back later on.'

'Good,' said Sybil. 'My husband will be here then and he'll doubtless want to talk to you.'

'Then I'll say good morning, ma'am, for the time being.'

'Good morning, Mr. Whittlebait. It's a pleasure to have you looking after us.'

10

The Face was Familiar

Tim returned an hour and a half later to find Sybil with a frilly apron over a sweater and flannel skirt, and the house full of the fragrance of coffee and bacon. 'Now this is what men get married for,' he said and plonked himself down at the sunlit table.

'I'm glad that point's cleared up,' said Sybil. 'Where are the coppers?'

'Down at the pier. I expect they'll be along pretty soon to ask us questions.'

'What did you tell them?'

'Just that we found a body on the pier. Simple statement of fact.'

'Very prudent. But you've been gone a long time.'

'Ran some errands,' said Tim through a mouthful of grapefruit. 'Got the papers and saw about connecting the phone and stopped at the post office to see if we could have mail delivered.'

'Can we?'

'No. Have to get it there. Damn nuisance. Here's something I've fetched for a start.' He tossed a letter across the table. 'It's addressed to you. From the war bride people, apparently.'

Sybil tore the envelope open and read the letter aloud: 'Dear War Bride, welcome to your new home. I always say there's nothing like a bit of mail to make one feel one's settled. I hope the handyman had the place ready for you in time. I forgot to mention on the phone that you'll have a neighbor named John Something; I'll look up before I mail this letter. A grumpy old party by all accounts, but harmless. He's the actual owner of your house, but we handle everything, and chances are you may not even meet him. I hear he hasn't set foot in the place since his wife died there a good many years ago. I'll pay you a visit one of these days and we can discuss any details that may come up. Yours for intercourse between nations, Mrs. Lemuel Barrelforth, President, New Jersey chapter

British-American War Brides Improvement Association.'

Sybil looked up. 'How very thoughtful. So that's what Mr. Squareless meant by unhappy memories. But I didn't think he was grumpy. Did you?'

'He acted a bit grumpy when the subject of his housekeeper came up.'

'Maybe she's his mistress. That would account for it.'

'Do you want to see the papers?' Tim said. They're full of our gambling war.'

'Oh yes. By all means.'

Tim went into the hall and came back with the *New York Times* and the *Daily News*. The former devoted its left-hand column to the story, presented with a distasteful holding-up of skirts, while the *News* screamed, 'Hunt Rival Big Shots in Gaming War.' The facts were much the same as the day before, except that it had been confirmed that Sam Magruder was the probable target of the Heinkel mob, and both he and Frankie Heinkel were wanted by the District Attorney's office for questioning. Said the *Times*: 'At a late hour this morning, both were still unavailable.' Said the *News*: 'At a late hour this morning, both were still on the lam.' Jacob Burlick, both papers reported, had been released on bail.

'The *Times* even has an editorial about it,' said Tim. 'It's entitled 'This Must Stop,' and it says it speaks for all decent people in calling upon the Mayor to take steps.'

'The *News* has one, too,' said Sybil. 'Different approach, though. It says this is what comes of repressing the healthy gambling instincts of the American people, and there should be a national lottery. Then it points out that one of the dead mobsters had a Russian name. And finally it says the whole business is the result of the war Roosevelt got us into.'

'It apparently speaks for the people the *Times* doesn't,' said Tim. 'Has it got any pictures?'

Sybil turned to the center spread. 'Lots,' she said. 'General view of the Breeze Club after the shooting, close-up of the bodies, a shot of our pal Jake — and look! Here's the table we were sitting at.'

Tim glanced at her. It struck him that her bright chatter sounded suddenly forced, the sort of chatter that sometimes breaks out after a funeral. He looked over her shoulder at the pictures. There was their table, all right, with an arrow pointing to it and a caption that read: 'Arrow indicates table at which Silky Sam sat with unidentified couple shortly before guns barked.'

'Isn't it exciting?' said Sybil. 'I think I'll cut it out and send it to England, with a note saying we're the little couple who isn't there.'

Again her voice seemed brittle and strained to Tim. Like Lady Macbeth coached by Noel Coward. He was silent for a moment, then said quietly, 'Sybil.'

'Yes, darling?' She smiled brightly.

'The chap on the pier — I told you he looked vaguely familiar.'

The expression and color left her face.

'I don't want to upset you, but I'm pretty sure it was Sam Magruder.'

She sat motionless, silent, her eyes staring past him into space.

'I'm sorry,' he began, then he stopped.

There was something in her drawn features that clicked. 'You knew it all the time?'

'When you lifted his hat.' She spoke almost inaudibly, still without looking at him.

There was a loud knocking at the door.

11

Open and Shut Case

'Sorry to trouble you folks,' said the Chief of Police of Bankville, a fat and red-faced and comfortable-looking man. 'Specially seein' you just moved in. But that's these Pinies for you. Inconsiderate.'

'Come in and have some coffee,' said Tim.

'Don't mind if I do,' said the Chief. 'Smells mighty good.'

'How about your colleague?'

'My what? Oh, Officer Jenkins. I left him on the pier. Somebody's got to watch the remains till Doc Medford gets there. Got to follow the rule book, even in a picayune open-and-shut case like this.' He lumbered into the dining room and sat. 'Now this is a real treat, ma'am,' he said to Sybil as she placed a steaming cup in front of him. Tim noticed that her hand was steady.

109

'Got to mix a little business with the pleasure, though,' the Chief went on. 'Don't reckon it'll take long.' He pulled a notebook from his pocket. 'Let's see, I've got your names and presumably this is your address we're sittin' in. All we need now is a few words how you happened to find the remains.'

'Perhaps my wife had better take over,' said Tim. 'She actually saw it first.'

'You don't mind, ma'am?'

'Not at all,' said Sybil coolly. 'I'd gone to the beach for a bit of a stroll before breakfast. It was a lovely morning, you know.'

'Real nice.' The Chief sipped his coffee.

'And I happened to glance up at the pier and saw a man's face peeking over the railing. That is, it looked as if he were peeking over. That startled me, because I'd expected the place to be deserted.'

'Naturally,' said the Chief.

'Then, when he didn't move or change expression, I thought something must be wrong. I came back to the house and called my husband and we went down together to have a look. There was the

110

body, and that's the story.'

The Chief scribbled. 'You didn't touch anything, of course.'

'No,' said Sybil. Her eyes met Tim's.

'And you'd never seen the fellow before? You couldn't have, being strangers.'

'Quite,' said Sybil.

The Chief closed his notebook with a sigh and put it in his pocket. 'Nice and simple so far,' he said. 'Hope it stays that way. These Pinies, you know, can give you one hell of a headache. It's not that they're any worse than most people, understand, but they're like these hill-billies you read about — they don't like outsiders poking into their affairs. Something happens, they shut up like clams. If one of 'em happens to beat his wife's brains out, he figures it's his business and nobody else's. I'd just as soon it was myself, but the law's the law.'

'You said a moment ago that it was an open-and-shut case,' said Tim. 'How do you mean that, exactly?'

'Suicide,' said the Chief with a ponderous shrug. 'That's how it looks. Fellow sat on the bench, pushed his hat back, shot himself, and let the gun fall into the water. Mind you, Doc Medford may decide different, but that's how I figure it.'

'Wait a minute,' said Tim. 'His hat was pushed back?'

'Yeah. Pushed right back.'

'It wasn't pushed back when I saw it.'

'Now, darling,' said Sybil, 'you were rattled and so was I. Our friend here is used to this sort of thing and it's all in a day's work to him. Right?'

'Right,' said the Chief. 'And speakin' of the day's work, I'd better be gettin' on with it.' He rose heavily and beamed at Sybil. 'This has been real nice, ma'am, real nice. As I said before, I hate to bother you with a thing like this. Worst of it is, I'll probably have to bother you again if there's an inquest, and I reckon there will be.'

'When?' asked Sybil.

'Depends. Got to get the body identified, and Doc Medford's got to make his report. Couple of days, most likely. You folks got a phone?'

'We have, but it's not connected yet,'

said Tim. 'I hope it will be in a day or so.'

'Well, I'll keep in touch,' said the Chief. 'And thanks for the coffee.' He straightened his rumpled blue coat and put his hat on as he moved sideways, like a plump crab, out of the room. A moment later they heard the sound of his car rolling down the driveway.

Tim looked at Sybil. 'Damned funny about the hat,' he said.

Sybil shrugged. 'I don't know,' she said. 'It's none of our business.'

'No? It's none of our business if there's a killer lurking around the premises?' He stopped short and sat up straight in his chair. 'My God, that may be it! The killer may have sneaked back to the pier and rearranged the hat. Maybe he was on the pier when we were. Maybe he heard me mention the hat.'

'Awfully far-fetched, darling,' said Sybil. 'You know what I think?'

'No, but I'd very much like to.'

'I think the police rearranged the hat themselves, to avoid a lot of unnecessary fuss.'

'Unnecessary to whom?'

'To all concerned.'

Tim drummed his fingers on the tablecloth. Then he said, 'Look, Sybil, let's not play guessing games with each other. There's no doubt in my mind that that body is Sam Magruder's. Apparently there's no doubt in yours, either. Did you hope I wouldn't recognize him?'

'Yes.'

'Why?'

'Because I knew you'd want to tell the police.'

'Why shouldn't I tell the police?'

'Because it would involve us in a great deal of unpleasantness.'

'You don't find it unpleasant to think there's a murderer in the neighborhood?'

'I don't think there is one in the neighborhood. Isn't it reasonable to suppose that Mr. Magruder was taken for a ride, as the gangster films say, and that the — the assassins drove him here because they wanted to dispose of the body in an out-of-the-way place?'

'Well, yes,' said Tim. 'I suppose.'

'You don't think they'd hang about, do you?'

'I don't know. In any case, why not tell the police?'

'You see,' she went on, 'it would be most unfortunate if my name should be publicly linked in any way with Mr. Magruder's death. Which it certainly would be if we told everything to the police. Because, inevitably, it would involve his acquaintance with my father.'

'You mean,' said Tim, 'it might reflect on your father's name?'

'More than that,' said Sybil, 'it might draw attention to his death.'

'I see,' said Tim, although he didn't.

'I didn't want to tell you this,' she said. 'It's over and done with. But my father didn't die a natural death. He was killed by an automobile.'

'Oh,' said Tim. He fumbled for suitable words. 'An accident?'

Sybil's voice grew hard and flat. 'No,' she said, 'it was intentional. He was murdered.'

She put her head down on the table and cried.

12

Father was a Merry Old Boy

Tim walked around the table and put a hand on Sybil's shoulder. Nothing happened, so he walked around the table again and said, 'There, there.' Sybil went on crying. He started around the table a third time, then realized with a jolt that a face was peering through the kitchen door.

'Who the hell are you?' he snapped.

The face looked injured and embarrassed. 'Elias Whittlebait, at your service.'

'Oh,' said Tim. 'Excuse me.'

'Ain't the missus well?' asked Mr. Whittlebait.

'She's a little upset.'

Mr. Whittlebait pursed his lips and looked sage. 'About that there — that there — ' He let his nasal voice trail off and nodded in the direction of the pier.

Sybil lifted her head and tried to smile.

116

'You go talk to Mr. Whittlebait,' she said to Tim. 'I'll be all right.'

'Let's go into the kitchen,' said Tim.

It was a relief to be talking about such solid matters as plumbing, storm windows, furnace care, and the weather. Mr. Whittlebait seemed to hold exceptionally sensible views on these and kindred subjects, including wages. Tim was charmed with him and sorry when the handyman descended to the basement with his valise of unlikely-looking tools.

Sybil's eyes were slightly swollen, but otherwise she appeared calm when Tim returned to the dining room. A little too calm, in fact. There was an impassivity in her face that Tim found vaguely disturbing. He touched her cheek experimentally, then sat again at the table. 'Feel better, dear?' he asked.

'Much.'

'Would you like to tell me about your father?'

'Why?'

Tim counted ten while he told himself that Sybil had been under a strain and he mustn't let himself get annoyed. 'I thought you'd like to get it off your chest,' he said.

'Off my chest? How unromantic.'

'Off your alabaster bosom, then.'

'That's better.' Again, that hard brightness. 'I'd hate to spoil your illusions about the nobility.'

'I'll risk it.'

'You'll risk finding out that even a lady with a capital L has feet of clay? Big feet, usually, though not in my case.'

With an effort, he kept his voice tender. 'Please tell me about it,' he said.

'Very well.' She spoke in a precise monotone, like a child forced against its will to recite for company. 'Daddy sailed for the United States in August of 1939 on the *Queen Alexandria*. The day he landed in New York, he was struck by a car in front of his hotel. The car didn't stop. Daddy was killed instantly. That's all.'

Tim waited a moment, then he asked, 'Why do you think it was intentional?'

'He told me. He told me before he left he might never come back.'

'Did he tell you why?'

118

'No. But I guessed.' She swallowed. 'I might as well finish. Daddy was in some sort of a mess. He loved to play cards for high stakes. He used to say he should have lived in the Restoration.' A faint fond smile crossed her face and vanished. 'On one of his trips — Daddy was quite a globe-trotter, too, you know — I think he must have lost a great deal more than he could afford. More, perhaps, than he could pay. And I think he felt it incumbent upon him, as a matter of honor, to face his creditors even though he knew them to be a ruthless gang of crooks. He knew what they might do, and they did.'

'Did you tell the authorities?'

'At the end of August, 1939?' said Sybil. 'Do you think any British authorities had time for a silly young girl's far-fetched murder theory? Even I didn't have time for it. But it was always in the back of my mind, all through the war. It always will be. Unless — I don't know what.'

Again Tim waited a bit before he spoke. 'Where does Sam Magruder fit in?'

'Daddy trusted Sam,' said Sybil softly. 'That I'm sure of. And I have a feeling he may have seen Sam before he went to his — to his last rendezvous. Whatever it was, Sam had something to tell me. Something I'll never know.'

Tim reached out and patted her hand. 'Sybil,' he said, 'don't misunderstand me. But did you expect to see Sam Magruder when you came to New York?'

She looked at him with eyes that narrowed a little. 'No,' she said. 'I'd forgotten all about him. Why?'

'I wondered. It was a pretty lucky coincidence, wasn't it?'

'Yes,' said Sybil. 'A very lucky coincidence. And just a coincidence. Are you suggesting it was something else?'

'I'm suggesting nothing,' said Tim. In spite of himself, the coldness of his voice matched hers. 'I'm about to, however.'

'Yes?'

'I suggest that we notify the police immediately that we have recognized the body of the man on the pier as that of Sam Magruder. And that we give them all the information and cooperation that we can.'

Sybil stared, then said, 'Don't be ridiculous.' She spoke with the iron lightness of a woman whose husband had just asked if her old evening dress wouldn't do another season.

'I fail to see why it's ridiculous,' said Tim.

'You fail to see a great many things,' said Sybil. The hard brightness cracked before her rising emotion. 'You fail to see what I've been through. What I'm going through. You don't care. You don't understand. You don't want to understand. You're a — a *pedant*.' She choked on her words.

'What?' shouted Tim, his own frayed temper suddenly giving way. 'By God, I'll be called a lot of things, but I'm damned if I'll be called a peasant. Not by capital L ladies or anybody else.' He stopped suddenly, realizing that Sybil was shaking with helpless laughter. 'What's so damned funny?'

'Not peasant, darling,' she gasped, 'not peasant. *Pedant*. With a D.'

'Oh,' said Tim. He laughed, too. It was suddenly the funniest thing in the world. They laughed till they cried. Their laughter billowed around them, sweeping away suspicion and anger in joyous, flooding relief.

Tim found he was holding her in his arms, her cheek wet against his, her lips salty on his.

122

13

Old Dog Tries New Tricks

In the early afternoon, John Squareless appeared at the front door. He wore his windbreaker again, the air having grown chill and the sunlight pale.

'Afraid you people will think I'm a busybody instead of a recluse,' he said to Sybil, who answered his knock.

'We prefer you as a busybody,' said Sybil. 'Do come in.' She led him into the living room where Tim, who had been making a half-hearted effort to straighten out his notes in the library, joined them.

Squareless sat in an easy chair and lit his pipe. 'Heard about the unpleasant discovery you two made this morning,' he said. 'Something of a shock, I should imagine.'

'A bit,' said Sybil. 'However, the police seem to have the situation well in hand.'

'Do they?' said Squareless. 'From what

I gather, the police are assuming it's a case of suicide on which they hope to close their books as soon as possible and get back to their checkers.'

'Have you any reason to think it's not a suicide, Mr. Squareless?' asked Sybil.

'Yes,' said Squareless, 'I do.' He puffed on his pipe a moment. 'I thought you two might have reached the same conclusion.'

'We did some speculating,' said Tim, 'but we didn't reach any conclusions.'

'After all,' said Sybil, 'who are we to pit ourselves against the guardians of the peace? Why do you think it wasn't suicide, Mr. Squareless?'

'Because a man who's going to commit suicide,' said Squareless, 'doesn't make a social event out of it. And there were several people roaming around the pier last night.'

'Really?' said Sybil.

'Yes,' said Squareless. He looked at her as if he expected her to say something more. But she only maintained her expression of bright interest.

Squareless studied his pipe. 'I'm a late sitter-upper,' he resumed. 'Books, I find, taste better at night. About two o'clock this morning, while I was teetering between the decline and fall of Rome, I happened to notice a light at the end of the pier. It came and went several times, as if somebody were using a flashlight rather cautiously. Of course, it could have been a fisherman, but somehow I didn't think it was. So I climbed into my dinghy for a little patrol work.'

Tim remembered the man in the boat and sucked in his breath. Squareless glanced at him.

'It was just top of the ebb,' he went on, 'so I was able to get pretty close to the pier. Close enough to make out two figures who seemed to be carrying something. I could hear 'em talking, too. You know how even a whisper carries across water. Of course, the sound of oars does, too, and first thing I knew a beam of light lit square on the boat. It flashed off right away, and there wasn't another peep from the pier. I stayed around for a bit, until the tide started in and took me along with it, but everything was quiet. Then suddenly I heard voices again, this

125

time at the foot of the pier. I was around the point and couldn't see anything, but I got the impression that somebody had interrupted the people I'd seen.'

'That was me,' said Tim. In the brief silence, he felt Sybil's eyes but didn't look at her.

'I thought so,' said Squareless. 'I'm glad you've seen fit to tell me.'

'It was my fault he didn't before,' said Sybil quickly. 'I have a horror of getting involved in anything of this sort.'

'As a recluse,' said Squareless, 'so do I. I don't propose to get involved, either. As far as I'm concerned, this conversation is strictly between the three of us.'

Again it seemed to Tim that he was inviting Sybil to further confidence.

'The three of us,' sighed Sybil. 'To a bridge player, the saddest of all words.'

'Did the chap on the pier look like a bridge player?' asked Squareless. There was nothing in his tone to suggest that this was intended as more than a grim pleasantry, and yet Tim couldn't help feeling that the question was loaded.

'He looked livelier than some partners

I've had,' said Sybil.

'Speaking of bridge,' said Squareless, apparently resigning himself to the change of subject, 'I must confess that our conversation of last night has reawakened my dormant appetite for the game.'

'Then let's do something drastic about a fourth,' said Sybil. 'Let's scour the highways and byways. I meant to ask the Police Chief this morning.'

'To play or to track down a player?' asked Tim.

'Whichever.'

'As a matter of fact,' said Squareless, 'there ought to be somebody in the Pinewoods community who either knows the rudiments of the game or could learn them. There's a little general store back there where they sit around the stove all winter and play some damned thing that involves a deck of cards. Pinochle, probably.'

A clang from the basement brought a sudden light to Sybil's face. 'We could ask Mr. Whittlebait!' she exclaimed.

'Who?' said Squareless. 'Oh, the handyman.'

Sybil went into the hall and opened the

door leading to the basement. 'Mr. Whittlebait,' she called.

'Be right up, ma'am,' said Mr. Whittlebait's voice from below. It could be heard continuing querulously, as he plodded up the stairs, 'Well, I hope that danged thing will work now. Done all I could. Ain't a professional plumber, you know.'

'I'm sure you've done your best, Mr. Whittlebait,' said Sybil, ushering him toward the living room. 'The big question now is, can you play bridge?'

'Played London Bridge as a kid,' said Mr. Whittlebait. 'London Bridge, Post Office, everything.' He winked at Tim.

Sybil looked despairingly at Squareless.

'But I reckon,' went on Mr. Whittlebait, 'you're talkin' about the card game.'

Hope flickered.

'Never played it myself. Heard folks talk about it a good bit.'

'Folks who live around here?' asked Sybil.

'Nah,' said Mr. Whittlebait. 'Summer people.'

'What sort of cards do you play?' asked Squareless. 'Seems to me I've seen you

128

taking a hand over at the store.'

'Yep,' said Mr. Whittlebait, 'I play a sociable game now and then. Pinochle mostly. Sometimes rummy. Sometimes five hundred.'

'Five hundred, eh?' said Squareless. 'By Jove, man, if you can play five hundred, you can learn bridge.'

'I'm a pretty old dog to be learnin' new tricks,' said Mr. Whittlebait. 'You folks got any more chores you want done?'

'We certainly do,' said Sybil briskly. 'We want you to sit right down and learn a new trick or two. You owe it to yourself, Mr. Whittlebait. Bridge is a great social asset, you know.'

Mr. Whittlebait twisted his cap in his hands and looked hesitantly around the room. Outside the green-curtained windows, the sky had grown overcast and a few drops of rain glistened on the panes. The long grass of the dunes bent in the wind.

'Right cozy in here,' he said. 'Wouldn't hurt to try, I don't suppose.'

Sybil rubbed her hands gleefully. 'This is marvelous,' she exclaimed. 'Fetch the

129

table, Tim, darling, there's a lamb.'

'If Sybil knew anything about American holidays,' observed Tim, 'I'd say she was celebrating the glorious Fourth.'

★　★　★

An hour and a half later, Mr. Whittlebait, chipper and bright-eyed, made his dozenth triumphant effort to take a trick with the right bower and received his dozenth reminder that while there might be bowers by Bendemeer's stream, there weren't any in bridge.

'Dangnation,' sighed Mr. Whittlebait. 'If I could just get them bowers out of my mind, I might get onto this game. It's got possibilities, I can see that much. But I got to be gettin' back to the store.'

'Why?' asked Sybil.

Mr. Whittlebait looked embarrassed. 'Promised some fellows I'd play pinochle,' he said. 'Sorry.'

'I should think so,' said Sybil.

Mild reproof entered Mr. Whittlebait's meek voice. 'I wouldn't of stayed this long, ma'am,' he said, 'except I thought it was takin' your mind off of — off of what had you so upset and high-stirical a while back.' He gave his head a virtuous little shake and took his departure.

Squareless stared at Sybil, sucking on his pipe. 'Sorry to hear you were upset,' he said.

'Oh, Mr. Whittlebait's exaggerating,' said Sybil. 'I was much more upset when he led away from his ace-queen three times running.'

'He's a pretty shrewd chap, though, at that,' said Squareless. 'I'm referring, of course, to his sense of cards.'

'Of course,' said Sybil. She rose and went into the hall. A couple of minutes later she came back and said, 'Damn! Mr. Whittlebait may have a sense of cards, but he certainly lacks a sense of plumbing.'

14

A Room with a View

The next morning, thanks to Mr. Whittlebait's ministrations, none of the toilets worked. There was an outdoor privy behind the garage, dating from the early years of the house, but this was a poor sort of silver lining on a gray and chill day with a hint of drizzle in the air.

'O Whittlebait, O Whittlebait, wherefore art thou, Whittlebait,' chanted Sybil bitterly. 'How does one get hold of our leprechaun, anyway?'

'He just appears,' said Tim. 'And that's a misquotation. Juliet wasn't wondering where Romeo was, she wondered why he was.'

'Why he was what?'

'Romeo.'

Sybil gave him an exasperated look. 'Why did I have to marry a professor?' she asked the ceiling. 'Why didn't I marry a plumber?'

'Did one ever ask you?'

'Dozens,' said Sybil. 'Furthermore, I was led to expect that American plumbing always worked.'

'Better take it up with the War Bride Association,' said Tim.

'I shall,' said Sybil. 'At the moment, though, I'd prefer to take it up with Mr. Whittlebait. Let's go ask Mr. Squareless if he knows how to reach him.'

'He'll probably turn up any minute,' said Tim. 'Besides, I get a distinct impression that Mr. Squareless doesn't encourage visitors.'

'He encourages me. I get the impression that he's very fond of me.'

'As who isn't?'

'This is no time for pretty sentiment,' said Sybil, although she smiled. 'Are the keys in the car?'

Tim nodded and Sybil rose from the breakfast table. 'I'll be back in a jiffy,' she said.

She climbed into the car and drove along the sandy road through the dunes. She swung into the macadam thorough-fare, which was deserted, luckily, because Sybil kept painstakingly to the left-hand side. The car rattled across the white bridge, then she saw a driveway entrance overgrown with catbriars and beach grass and a sign that said: Private. No Trespassing.

She turned into the driveway, the briars catching at the fenders, and almost immediately encountered another sign that said: Trespassers Will Be Prosecuted. Twenty yards further along, still another sign rose truculently from the bayberry to say: Trespassers Will Positively Be Prosecuted.

Sketchy though her familiarity with American advertising methods was, Sybil half expected a final sign that would say: Unless They Use Burma Shave.

However, there were no more signs. Instead, a stone wall, about six feet high, suddenly appeared, dipping through the dunes, which it almost matched in color. Apparently it sliced across the point, isolating the tip, without being visible from the other side of the inlet. There was a weather-beaten wooden gate in it, at which the road ended. Beyond the wall, Sybil could see the tall brown walls of the house, its shingle roof sagging between a forlorn cupola and a shaky turret.

She got out of the car and tried the gate, but it was evidently bolted. *Well*, thought Sybil, *he's barged in on us a couple of times. And this is an emergency.* She clambered to the fender of the car and onto the hood, from where it was an easy vault across the gate.

She landed with a bit of a jolt in the gravel on the other side and immediately she heard the loud barking of a dog. Across the wet, shaggy lawn in front of the house bounded a big German shepherd, looking as if it had leaped straight out of *Red Riding Hood*.

'Down, sir!' cried Sybil. Her voice was authoritative, but she felt cold sweat breaking out. She remembered the old theory that dogs can smell fear.

The shepherd stopped, ears lifted, tail stiff, eyes suspicious. Sybil took a step and the dog took a step.

'Down, sir,' she said again. 'Enough of this gavotte.'

The dog didn't move. Sybil wondered uneasily what to do next. Then, to her relief, a deep female voice called from the direction of the house, 'Here, Gertie, come here!'

The shepherd looked around, then reluctantly, its bloodshot eyes lingering, it turned and loped toward the front door.

In the doorway, between scraggly rose-bushes, an elderly woman stood. She was tall and her face was gaunt and severe. At the moment, her hair was caught up in a duster and she wore an apron over a shapeless house-dress. She was holding a mop, much as an ancient sentry might have held a pikestaff. 'Yes?' she said. 'What is it?'

'I'm looking for Mr. Squareless,' said Sybil.

The woman stared at her, thinking this over. The dog squatted on its haunches beside the stone steps. Sybil became irritably aware of the fine, cold rain against her face.

Then Squareless himself, wearing a purple smoking-jacket over an open white shirt, appeared in the doorway. 'All right, Julia,' he said. 'I'll take care of this.'

The woman didn't move for a moment. Then she bent her head toward Squareless and apparently whispered something to him.

'Yes,' said Squareless roughly, 'yes, yes.'

The woman looked at Sybil, and an expression of interest and of something like pity touched her features. Then she gave a shrug and disappeared into the house.

Sybil picked her way across half-buried flagstones, the long grass wet around her ankles. 'Good morning,' she said, trying to sound casual and amiable.

'Good morning,' said Squareless. His broad shoulders almost filled the doorway and he made no move to stand aside.

'Your dog gave me a bit of a fright,' said Sybil.

'That's the dog's job.'

'Funny job for a dog named Gertie,' said Sybil.

'The name isn't Gertie. It's Goethe.'

'Oh.'

Squareless remained motionless in the doorway. Sybil turned up the collar of her tweed coat. 'It's raining, you know,' she said sweetly.

'You mean you want to come in?'

'I expect to be asked.'

'All right,' said Squareless. There was no expression on his face or in his voice. 'Come in, then.'

He stood back from the door and she stepped into a completely bare hall, no rugs, no hangings, just a staircase and beyond it a naked glass door opening onto a bleak veranda, and beyond that the gray ocean.

'Cozy,' said Sybil.

'Isn't it?' said Squareless. 'Wait here a minute.' He opened a door and went through it, closing it behind him. Two or three minutes passed while she stood there, shivering a little in the creeping chill. Then the door opened again and Squareless said, 'This way, please.'

She walked into a room that made her catch her breath — a room so full of things, so warm, so deeply lived in that it seemed it must belong to a different house, a different part of the world. It was a big room shaped like half an oval, its outermost curve occupied by great bellying casement windows hung in heavy draperies of dark red. A thick carpet of dimly mellow Oriental design covered most of the floor. Facing the windows was a massive fireplace of yellowish stone, surmounted by a mantelpiece of polished wood that Sybil thought was teak. Of the

138

same wood was a huge carved desk that sat in the curve of the windows, cluttered with books and papers and pipes and curious paperweights.

The remaining wall space was devoted to bookshelves, between the tops of which and the ceiling were ranged the heads of a variety of animals: caribou, wildebeest, and bear, among others. Over the fireplace hung the glass-eyed majesty of a lion. Interspersed among the heads were weapons of all sorts: bows and arrows and primitive spears, long-barreled pistols with ornate bone stocks, and an old flintlock next to a Mauser.

In all this richly bewildering room there were only two chairs: one a solid, square affair behind the desk; the other a spacious easy chair of natural leather that sat beside the fireplace with a red hassock in front of it. A brazier of coals glowed in the fireplace.

'Sit down,' said Squareless, gesturing toward the easy chair.

Sybil hesitated. 'It's so obviously your chair,' she said. 'I'd feel like an intruder sitting there.'

139

'You are an intruder,' said Squareless. 'You might as well feel like one.'

He lifted a brass tray containing coffee things from a taboret and carried it to the door. 'Julia,' he called. 'Some fresh coffee.' He handed the tray through the door, then crossed the room and sat behind the desk. 'Don't stand there,' he said. 'It makes me nervous.'

Sybil smiled and sank into the easy chair, stretching her feet on the hassock. 'A bit of all right, this,' she remarked. 'It's a wonderful room.'

'I like it.'

'My father would have liked it. He loved to travel and collect faraway things.'

'The late Earl?'

Sybil glanced up in surprise. 'Yes,' she said. 'How did you know?'

'The war bride people mentioned it. Added inducement, I suppose.'

'No doubt,' said Sybil. She realized, then, why the fat red volume on the desk in front of him was familiar: *Burke's Peerage. Oh ho*, she thought, *the old boy's been checking up*.

Squareless saw the direction of her gaze

and, rather abruptly, changed the subject. 'You know,' he said, 'you're the first woman to have entered this room in a great many years.'

'Except for your housekeeper, surely.'

'Naturally.'

'Julia,' said Sybil musingly. 'I once had a nanny named Julia.'

'Indeed? How remarkable.'

'It's remarkable that I should remember it,' said Sybil, flushing slightly at his sarcastic tone. 'Because I don't remember anything else about her.'

The housekeeper entered the room at that moment with the tray, from which fragrant vapor arose. 'Where shall I put it?' she asked.

'Where you usually put it,' said Squareless.

She placed the tray on the little round table and asked, 'Shall I pour?'

'Don't bother. Our guest is able-bodied.'

The housekeeper looked at Sybil as if she would have liked to say something reassuring. Then her stern features hardened again and she left the room.

'Pour the coffee while it's hot,' said

Squareless. 'None for me, thanks. Had three cups already.'

He watched her while she poured, his thick fingers drumming on the desk. Behind him, the rain slanted against the leaded windowpanes. 'Well,' he said presently, 'to what do I owe this honor?'

'To an emergency,' said Sybil. 'None of our water closets work.'

'Oh,' said Squareless. 'Upstairs, second door on your left.'

'The emergency isn't so great as all that,' said Sybil. 'But I would like to get hold of Mr. Whittlebait as soon as possible. I thought perhaps you could tell me how one goes about finding these Pinies, as you call them.'

'I can tell you how one goes about it, but I can't guarantee results. One goes to the general store back in the woods, and if one's lucky, one finds whom one's looking for. Otherwise, there's usually someone who'll fetch him.'

'I see,' said Sybil. 'And how does one find the general store?'

'It's on the other side of the marshes, where the high ground begins in the cedar swamps. Take the first road to the west and stick with it. You'll think it's disappearing under you, but it'll take you there.'

'Thank you,' said Sybil. She sipped her coffee, then asked, 'If I do run Mr. Whittlebait to earth, could I interest you in another bridge session?'

For the first time that morning, Squareless's expression relaxed. He actually chuckled. 'You know,' he said, 'gruesome though it was, I rather enjoyed it.'

'So did I,' said Sybil, 'in a masochistic way. Why don't you drop by after lunch?'

'I might.'

In spite of his brusqueness, she got the impression, as Tim had earlier, that he wanted very much to come, but for some reason was hesitant. 'I do hope you will,' she said. She finished her coffee and stood up.

'Wait a minute,' said Squareless. 'There's something I want to show you.' He also arose, pushing his chair back. 'Have you noticed the view from these windows?' His voice was amiable enough, but the question, somehow, wasn't. So a conversational hangman might have asked, 'Have you ever seen a knot like this?'

'Why, no,' said Sybil. 'Not particularly.'

'Take a look,' said Squareless.

She walked around the desk, hiding her uneasiness with a look of polite interest, and stood beside him in the embrasure.

'It's a bit blurred at the moment,' said Squareless, 'but you can easily imagine what a vista it would be on a clear day. A day like yesterday, for example.'

'Quite,' said Sybil. He was standing close to her, smelling cleanly of soap and shaving lotion and tobacco. His shoulder, in the velvet jacket, almost touched hers as he leaned toward her to point toward the opposite bluff.

'You can just make out the end of the pier there,' he said. 'But yesterday it was as distinct as my own lawn. I could see everything that moved there, and one thing that didn't move.'

Sybil was silent, waiting.

'I saw a young woman alone on the pier. Alone except for the thing that didn't move. She seemed strangely interested in that thing. Why?' He looked straight at her, his rugged features like granite, and yet it seemed to her that his eyes were troubled.

She turned away from his gaze. 'I'm sorry,' she said. 'I don't know what you're talking about.'

'Did you recognize him?'

'I still don't know what you're talking about.'

'Yes, you do.' His voice was harsh, but harsh with an effort, as if it pained him. 'You know exactly what I'm talking about.'

He put his hand on her arm and she drew it quickly away. 'Please,' she said.

'You've got to confide in someone,' he said. 'Why won't you confide in me?'

Sybil lifted her chin and faced him. 'I have no need to confide in anyone,' she said. Their eyes met, hers defiant, his grimly regretful. 'I must go,' she added. 'Will Goethe let me pass?'

'I'll come with you,' said Squareless.

They passed through the empty hall and across the ragged, wet lawn in silence. Goethe appeared from the tangled rosebushes and trotted beside them to the gate.

15

Babes in the Pine Woods

Tim was at work in the library when she returned. He hadn't heard her come in, evidently, and for a moment she watched him through the French doors. His elbows rested on the desk, one hand running back and forth through his rumpled hair. He looked at once boyish and scholarly, absorbed in the litter of papers in front of him.

A tender and rather sad little smile touched Sybil's lips as she watched him. Then she crossed the living room, tapped on the glass door, and opened it. 'Nose to grindstone,' she said. 'That's what I like to see.'

He grinned up at her. 'I went down in the cellar to look at the plumbing,' he said, 'and a Ph.D. thesis seemed so simple by comparison that I started right in.'

'I'll leave you to it, then,' said Sybil.

'Mr. Squareless told me how to find Mr. Whittlebait.'

'How?'

'One goes to some sort of store back in the woods and whistles.'

'I'd better come with you.'

'You needn't. Unless you want to.'

'I want to, all right. I'm bogged down in notes I can't read any more.'

They found the road to the west without any difficulty, but it was a good thing Squareless had mentioned its tendency to disappear or they might have abandoned it. Once outside of the town, it became little more than a couple of sandy ruts running through the brown marsh grass toward the thick gloom of the cedar swamps. The gray light deepened as they drove through the cedars, rising from pools half-hidden in the underbrush. Then the needle-carpeted pine woods began.

Almost immediately they came to a circular clearing on one side of which sat, unmistakably, the general store. It was a small ramshackle building with a corrugated tin roof and smoke coming out of a rusted metal chimney. Its two front windows were plastered with signs that announced everything from last year's county fair to next year's Miss Rheingold. Cases of empty beer and pop bottles were stacked against one end of it.

Across the way was a sagging frame house with a fence of sporadic pickets around it. Chickens pecked aimlessly about the bare yard and a couple of smeary children sat huddled in the door. Through the dark green trees other houses were visible here and there, shacks really, some of corrugated tin, some of wood and tarpaper and, possibly, string and safety pins.

'This, I take it, is the native village,' said Tim.

'Looks hostile,' said Sybil. 'We should have brought some glass beads.'

Tim parked the car beside the store and they approached the front door in which cardboard substituted for glass. 'Do we knock?' asked Sybil.

'Don't see why,' said Tim. 'It's public.'

He pushed the door open and they walked inside. A strong smell of kerosene, of tobacco in its less lovely forms, and of damp clothing met them with a steamy rush. A counter ran the length of the room, which was lit by a bare and dangling bulb, and there were glass cases at each end with candy bars and chewing gum in them. Behind it, with his hat on, the middle-aged storekeeper, wearing a soiled apron over a blue turtleneck sweater, was figuring out the purchases of a woman dressed in a man's mackinaw.

Beside the pot-bellied stove in the middle of the room sat half a dozen men playing cards. Two of them sat on kitchen chairs and the rest on upturned boxes. A flat piece of beaverboard, resting on two boxes, served as a table. The men were dressed much as Mr. Whittlebait and, for that matter, the corpse on the pier had been dressed. They all had either a hat or a cap on.

Everybody looked up as Tim and Sybil entered, suspicious eyes landing on the strangers with an impact almost physical. Then quickly the various pairs of eyes were lowered or turned away, no one looking directly at them, but all watchful, studying.

The storekeeper slowly put his stub of a pencil behind his ear. 'How do,' he said. He sounded wary, but ready to be cordial if it seemed advisable.

'How do,' said Tim pleasantly. 'We're looking for Mr. Whittlebait.'

'Ah, Mr. Whittlebait,' said the storekeeper. 'Then you'd be Mr. and Mrs. Ludlow.'

'That's right,' said Tim.

'Well, I tell you,' said the storekeeper thoughtfully, 'Mr. Whittlebait lives back in the woods a ways, but there's no sense you trompin' through the rain just to find him. He'll be along here any minute, so why don't you just make yourselves comfortable and wait for him?'

'Okay,' said Tim.

'Thank you,' said Sybil. She strolled to the counter and idly examined a pyramid of canned goods next to one of the glass cases. Tim watched the card game. Apparently it was pinochle, which he didn't understand.

The storekeeper finished his calculations on the back of a paper bag and the woman paid him out of a worn purse and

150

started to go. Her arms were full of bundles and she had trouble reaching for the doorknob. Tim opened it for her and felt the disapproval of the card players turned on him. The woman looked surprised and didn't say anything.

Tim walked back to the counter beside Sybil, and the storekeeper edged toward them. 'Hear you folks found a cadaver on the pier,' he said respectfully. 'Kind of a shock, I guess. Especially for the lady.'

'The lady was in London all through the blitz,' said Tim, 'and it takes a good deal to shock her.'

'That so?' said the storekeeper. He looked at Sybil admiringly. Sybil concentrated modestly on a can of beans.

The storekeeper turned back to Tim. 'Seems to have been a case of suicide,' he went on. 'Terrible thing. Can't understand it. He was such a nice, quiet sort of fellow.'

There was a sharp thud as Sybil dropped the can of beans. The faces around the card table looked up quickly. Sybil managed a feeble laugh and said, 'Butterfingers.' Then she picked up the

151

can and put it back on the pyramid with care.

'You knew him, did you?' asked Tim, trying hard to keep his own voice casual.

'Well, I did and I didn't,' said the storekeeper. 'He was a man kept pretty much to himself. Fact is, I don't even know his name. All I know is he lived somewhere in the woods and come here for his vittles. One of these old-timers, I guess; outlived his folks and didn't see much sense makin' new friends at his time of life. Folks get like that in the woods.'

'I see,' said Tim. 'Had he lived around here long?' Before the storekeeper could answer, the door opened and Elias Whittlebait walked in.

It was obvious that Mr. Whittlebait cut something of a swathe in his own bailiwick. He didn't put doeskin gloves into a Homburg and hand them to anybody, but it was that kind of an entrance. There was a commotion among the card players as they moved around to make room for him, and everybody said: 'Mornin', Elias,' and 'What say, Elias?'

and similar greetings of a respectful nature.

'Mornin', everybody,' said Mr. Whittlebait, bowing in all directions. Then he saw Tim and Sybil and his manner grew subtly deferential, at the same time making it plain that they were aliens. 'Well,' he said, 'what brings you folks back country?'

'You, Mr. Whittlebait,' said Sybil.

'Bet I know what it's about, too,' said Mr. Whittlebait, chuckling roguishly. 'It's about that there — ' He stepped toward them and lowered his voice. ' — that there commode.'

'Them there commodes,' corrected Sybil. 'They're all on the blink, now.'

'Do tell,' said Mr. Whittlebait. 'Still, it don't surprise me.' So might a Secretary of State have resignedly learned that his peace policy had failed in a wicked world. 'What you folks need,' he went on, 'is a genuine plumber. Don't worry about hurtin' my feelings. It's like I was your family doctor and something happened you needed a specialist for. Same thing exactly.'

'Can you recommend a specialist?' asked Tim.

Mr. Whittlebait considered. 'For a job like this one,' he said thoughtfully, 'I reckon Timkins is your best man. If it was an outside job, I'd say Bassett, but for this particular one, give me Timkins. That's Timkins over to Bankville.'

'Could we phone him from here?' asked Sybil.

''Fraid not, ma'am,' said Mr. Whittlebait.

From a back room came a whirring ring. Sybil raised her eyebrows and the storekeeper said, 'There goes that dratted alarm clock again.' He went into the back room.

'We might as well drive over to Bankville,' said Tim.

'I suppose so,' said Sybil. 'Thank you, Mr. Whittlebait. And if you'd like another go at bridge, drop around this afternoon.'

Mr. Whittlebait glanced with embarrassment at the card players but he also looked flattered. 'Well, now,' he murmured, 'I might at that. Like you say, it's a social asset.'

'Good,' said Sybil. 'We'll be looking for you.'

They walked back to the car in silence. Tim was waiting for Sybil to comment, but it was not until they had emerged from the woods into the marshland, hazy with the fine rain, that she spoke. 'Well,' she said lightly, 'it looks as if we were mistaken, doesn't it?'

'I'd like to think so,' said Tim. 'I don't, though.'

'What other explanation is there?'

'That Magruder had a hideaway somewhere around here.'

'But why?'

'Because somebody was after him. Somebody who finally got him.'

'Somehow,' said Sybil pensively, 'I can't think of Sam Magruder as running away to the woods to hide from anybody. It doesn't sound like him.'

'It's nothing against him,' said Tim. 'Lots of good people have done it. Seems to me there was an English king who actually hid in a tree.'

'Possibly,' said Sybil. 'But it still doesn't sound like Sam Magruder.'

Tim felt irritation crawling over him again. He shrugged and let the subject drop.

Bankville, in spite of the drizzle, looked comparatively cheerful after the desolation of Merry Point and the pine woods. People in raincoats or carrying umbrellas scurried along the pavements; and the stores, soda fountains, and eating-places looked cozy behind their rain-blurred windows.

As they drove along Main Street, they heard a police whistle, and both turned to see their friend the Chief waving at them. Tim stopped the car and he came toward them at a dog-trot, or, more accurately, a panda-trot. He rested his elbows on the window frame beside Tim, puffing and beaming under a black rubber hood.

'Wondered how I was going to get in touch with you folks,' he panted. 'Wanted to let you know the inquest's all set for tomorrow. Two o'clock. Hope you don't mind.'

'Not at all,' said Sybil, smiling at him. 'Have there been any developments?'

'Routine developments, that's all. Doc

Medford's report shows it must have been suicide, all right.'

'Must have been?' repeated Tim.

The Chief looked faintly annoyed. 'Well, it didn't show any reason to think it wasn't,' he said. 'That's good enough for me.'

'And that makes it good enough for us,' said Sybil.

'Thank you, ma'am,' said the Chief. 'We got him identified, too. More or less, anyhow.'

'Who was the poor chap?' asked Sybil.

'Like I figured, one of these Pinies. Two or three of 'em knew him by sight. Lived back there all by himself, apparently.'

'Had he lived there long?' asked Tim.

Again the Chief looked mildly annoyed. 'Long enough, I guess. These pine woods people don't keep track of time.'

'My stomach does,' said Sybil, 'and it tells me it's time for lunch.'

'See you tomorrow,' said the Chief, waving them on. 'Take care of yourselves.'

16

Whittlebait Wins a Bet

They decided to have lunch at the red-brick hotel with the potted shrubs in front of it. First, though, they unearthed Timkins, the plumber, and Timkins said he'd be over either late that afternoon or next morning. After lunch they did a spot of shopping and looked in at the post office, all of which made Tim feel like a burgher of the community. It was a feeling he enjoyed, for a change.

It was almost two when they got back to Merry Point. After the rain and the chill, the house, as they entered the hall-way, felt warm and soothing.

'Darling,' cried Sybil, 'isn't it good to be home! Let's jump straight into bed for the afternoon.'

A loud and disapproving harrumph crackled out of the living room. Standing in front of the fireplace was a tall, broad-bosomed woman dressed in sensible tweeds and large sensible shoes. A sensible hat was perched on her head. Her face, if you discounted its present expression, was not altogether unhandsome, but the features were large; and her complexion, which might have been a robust pink in earlier years or better weather, was a rawish red.

'Lumme!' cried Sybil. 'Who are you?'

The tall woman thrust her shoulders smartly back, which thrust her bosom less smartly forward, and said, 'I am Mrs. Lemuel Barrelforth, President of the New Jersey chapter of the British-American War Brides Improvement Association. I am sorry if I seem to be intruding.'

'On the contrary,' said Sybil. 'We're delighted to see you.'

'Rubbish,' snapped Mrs. Barrelforth. 'I was a war bride myself once, and rainy afternoons were just as wonderful then as they are now.' She sighed briefly and went on. 'However, here I am, and you'll have to make the best of it. I've come all the way from Trenton to look you over.'

'Where is Trenton?' asked Sybil.

'That's the sort of thing the New Jersey chapter proposes to teach you. Trenton is the capital of the state, population one hundred and twenty-four thousand, six hundred and ninety-seven, last census. Situated on the Delaware River, scene of George Washington's historic crossing, and too blasted far from here for convenience.'

'Oh,' said Sybil. 'Then you must be tired. Do sit down and I'll fetch you some tea. Or would you prefer coffee?'

'I'd prefer Scotch and plain water,' said Mrs. Barrelforth. She sat in one of the easy chairs, managing, in spite of its springy depth, to give an impression of being bolt upright.

'Let's all have Scotch,' said Sybil. 'It's a wonderful afternoon for drinking, too.'

'No ice,' Mrs. Barrelforth called after Tim as he headed dutifully for the pantry.

When he came back with a laden tray, Mrs. Barrelforth was saying to Sybil, 'So you see, my dear, the organization is national in scope and has no other purpose than to further the interests of those poor bewildered lassies far from home.'

'I'm not poor and bewildered,' said Sybil.

160

'So you're not,' agreed Mrs. Barrelforth, 'which is all the more reason why you should become a pillar of the organization rather than a supine recipient of its many benefits. We are talking,' she explained, turning to Tim, 'about the British-American War Brides Improvement Association, its principles and its purposes.'

'So I gathered,' said Tim, pouring whisky into glasses. 'Is that about right?'

'Mmm,' said Mrs. Barrelforth, peering. 'A bit niggardly. That's better.' She accepted the drink and turned back to Sybil. 'As I was saying, my dear, the fact that you are neither poor nor bewildered, plus the fact, if you don't mind my mentioning it, of your having borne a noble name, makes you a natural rallying point for those less fortunate than yourself. That's not bad Scotch. Where do you get it?'

'A recherché little place called Macy's,' said Tim.

'Oh,' said Mrs. Barrelforth. 'I ask because that's the sort of question the brides are constantly putting to the Association. It's often the first question. Here in Jersey, of course, it's no great problem, but I don't

161

know how our Kansas chapter handles it. Imagine some poor chit of a girl who's spent half her life in the bar parlor of the Goat and Grapes arriving in dry and cyclone-swept Kansas. Well, that's what the Association's for. Here's to it.'

They all drank to the Association.

'Take another example,' said Mrs. Barrelforth. 'Here's an innocent English maid who succumbs to some dashing southern major's talk of a plantation back home. She gets here, and what does she find? A couple of piano boxes nailed together in the Kentucky hills. That's the signal for our Kentucky chapter to step into the picture. They teach her to play the guitar, teach her to square dance, teach her to drink from a jug. In short, to adjust herself. Here's to the Kentucky chapter.'

They all drank to the Kentucky chapter.

'But what would I do,' asked Sybil, 'if I became a pillar of the organization?'

'Depends on the sort of pillar you want to be,' said Mrs. Barrelforth. 'Some pillars merely lend their names for letterhead purposes, others throw themselves heart and soul into the Association's activities

— meeting bride ships, distributing instructive booklets, finding apartments, giving cocktail parties, and holding classes in the American way of life. You know, how to eat corn on the cob, who the Dodgers are, and so on. In one or two cases, they've gone bail.'

'Sounds rather exhausting,' said Sybil. 'Isn't there any happy medium of pillarhood?'

'There probably is,' said Mrs. Barrelforth, 'but I was hoping you'd be the heart-and-soul type. That's what the Association needs. Don't forget, the Association provides these wide-eyed young strangers with a bridge to — '

'Heavens!' cried Sybil. 'I forgot to ask you if you played bridge.'

'No,' said Mrs. Barrelforth firmly. 'Don't play and don't approve. As I was saying, the Association provides — '

'It seems to me,' said Sybil, 'that it should provide bridge-loving brides with the necessary fourth.'

'Brides are supposed to be satisfied with a second,' said Mrs. Barrelforth. 'They need only one bid in life: two hearts.'

'It's nice to have an intervening bid of a diamond,' said Sybil. 'I'm sorry you disapprove of bridge, because we're expecting to have a game this afternoon.'

'Then perhaps I'd best be on my way,' said Mrs. Barrelforth. 'Did I hear somebody say 'One for the road'?'

'Absolutely,' said Tim, taking her empty glass.

'How are you getting back?' asked Sybil. 'I didn't see a car outside.'

'I came by train,' said Mrs. Barrelforth. 'Train to Bankville and then took a taxi. Extravagant but a legitimate expense. I'd better phone for another one.'

'Afraid the phone doesn't work,' said Tim.

'Damnation!' cried Mrs. Barrelforth. 'I should have known it, too, because I tried to get you this morning. Blast, that does pose a problem.'

'I can run you over to Bankville,' said Tim. He glanced out the window and so did their guest. The wind had come up and was driving the rain against the glass in splashing sheets. The ocean was a mass of angry foam-yellow crests amid the gray, and the afternoon sky hung darkly close to the earth.

'It's a frightful imposition,' murmured Mrs. Barrelforth.

'It's a frightful day to travel,' said Sybil. 'Why don't you stay the night? We've loads of room, and Tim can drive you to Bankville in the morning.'

'Good idea,' said Tim, trying to remember how much Scotch there was.

'Oh, I couldn't,' protested Mrs. Barrelforth, but with such a lack of conviction that she had to chuckle. 'If anybody asks me why I couldn't, I'd be stumped.'

'Splendid,' said Sybil. 'I'll slip upstairs right now and get your room ready.'

'Let me help,' said Mrs. Barrelforth.

'Nonsense,' said Sybil. 'You sit here and give my husband a little talk on the care and feeding of war brides.'

She went into the hall and up the broad, sagging stairs. The upstairs hall was a gray murk, considerably chillier than the floor below, and the wind rattled the windows behind the closed doors. Sybil shivered slightly and turned on all the lights in the room she intended for

Mrs. Barrelforth.

There were four large bedrooms, two on either side of the hall, with bathrooms between them at either end. Tim and Sybil had decided to close off the two rooms on the north side of the house while they used the southeastern one, with its big windows opening on the sea, as their own. The adjoining bedroom had been requisitioned by Sybil as a dressing room because, she explained, there was nothing less romantic than the sight of a wife in a slip and stockinged feet doing messy things to her face.

However, it seemed the lesser part of hospitality to offer Mrs. Barrelforth one of the closed-off bedrooms, which were musty and dank, so Sybil resignedly made up the bed in her dressing room. She'd skip the cold cream that night.

When she returned to the living room, she found that Squareless and Mr. Whittlebait had appeared and, since they had both known Mrs. Barrelforth by correspondence, the introductions had developed into a kind of old home week. It was a very restrained old home week, though, at least on the part of the new arrivals. Mr. Whittlebait, twisting his cap, seemed uncertain of his social status, and Squareless's frown said plainly that he should have been told there'd be strangers present.

'Would anybody like tea?' asked Sybil. 'Or shall we all stick to Scotch?'

'I'd like some tea,' said Squareless. 'And I'd like it laced with something. Rum, if you've got it — and if you've got Scotch, you probably have.'

'The weather bein' what it is,' said Mr. Whittlebait, 'I'll have the same. Medicinal, you might say.'

'The least I can do,' said Mrs. Barrelforth, getting up, 'is to make the tea. If you'll just show me the kitchen, my dear, then you can settle down to your cards. The devil's picture book, I call them.'

Sybil led her to the kitchen. Tim, while he was setting up the table, said conversationally to Mr. Whittlebait, 'I hear this poor fellow on the pier was a neighbor of yours.'

'So they tell me,' said Mr. Whittlebait, 'but I can't rightly place him. Storekeeper says he used to come in the store now and again, so I must of seen him. But he never hung round.' He grinned feebly and added, 'Guess he couldn't have been a card player.'

'Who couldn't have been a card player?' asked Sybil, returning from the kitchen.

'Fellow you found on the pier,' said Mr. Whittlebait.

'Who said he was a card player?' The question shot sharply from her lips, too sharply to be covered by the indifference of the smile she quickly put on. There was a strained silence. Tim saw both Squareless and Mr. Whittlebait looking at her curiously.

Then Mr. Whittlebait said mildly, 'Why, nobody, ma'am. Nobody said he was a card player.'

'Sybil's always on the lookout for a fourth,' said Tim. 'Shall we cut?' He spread the cards and the momentary tension melted.

Mr. Whittlebait cut the ace of spades. 'Looks like my lucky day,' he observed. 'Can you play this here game for nickels and dimes?'

'One can,' said Squareless, 'but it

168

would hardly be fair.'

'I don't mind, if you're thinkin' of me,' said Mr. Whittlebait. 'We generally play for a little something back at the store. Makes it more interestin', I always say.'

'I always say so, too,' said Sybil. 'Let's make it a twentieth. Then nobody can win or lose enough to worry about.'

'You couldn't win or lose much at this game anyhow, could you?' asked Mr. Whittlebait. 'I mean, not like at pinochle.'

'At one time, Whittlebait,' said Squareless, 'your opinion was shared by most of the gentry who make their living at the green baize. But when they saw what a chap named Culbertson could make out of it, without even using reflectors, a lot of them changed their minds. A fact, I might add, which I learned the hard way.'

'I'll be clanged,' said Mr. Whittlebait. 'And here I was figurin' it was kind of a sissy game.'

'Sissy like tossing the caber,' grunted Squareless. 'Your deal, Whittlebait.'

They settled down to the game. Mrs. Barrelforth came back with tea and a bottle of rum and proceeded to refresh everybody, including herself — and that substantially. She stood behind Mr. Whittlebait and watched the play for a while with that look of concentrated exasperation peculiar to the uninitiated, then subsided rather grumpily to her Scotch and some knitting she'd brought along.

It was more like a real bridge game than the previous day's had been. Mr. Whittlebait had finally turned apostate from his beloved right and left bowers and, though he wasn't precisely brilliant, he ploughed earnestly along and appeared, in an apologetic way, to be enjoying himself. After two cups of well-laced tea, his watery eyes behind their lenses grew squirrel-bright.

The wind roared round the house and the rain beat on the gradually darkening windows, while, like a steady accompaniment of kettle drums, the pounding of the ocean rose and fell. Inside, the green curtains were drawn, the lamps lit, and the fire crackling, and the only flaw in the general coziness lay in the un-American lack of plumbing facilities. Mrs. Barrelforth took the matter particularly to heart, not only because she had to make several trips outside, but because it was the sort of thing, she said, the Association should have looked after.

Toward six, Squareless looked at his watch and said he'd have to be getting along. Mr. Whittlebait expressed surprise at the passage of time and said he ought to be getting along, too, but being sixty cents behind, he'd be willing to play another hand or two.

'Let's make it the last one, then,' said Squareless.

'Good,' said Mrs. Barrelforth from her corner. 'If I'm to be allowed, at last, to join the party, I'll slip upstairs and powder. Which is no euphemism, worse luck.'

She went out, taking her glass with her, and Tim dealt the cards.

'Let's hope it's a lively hand,' said Sybil. 'And do try to remember about finesses, Mr. W.'

'Yes, ma'am,' said Mr. Whittlebait, who was her partner.

'Pass,' said Tim sourly. He had been holding rotten cards all afternoon.

'Maybe you're lucky in love,' said Mr. Whittlebait slyly.

'Obviously,' said Tim.

'I'm glad somebody in the family is,' said Sybil. She looked at her hand and felt a glow of pleasure. She had six hearts to the ace queen and five diamonds to the same combination, no spades and, in clubs, the ace and a small one. It was too good to entrust to Mr. Whittlebait's erratic responses. 'Four hearts,' she said.

Squareless passed without expression. Mr. Whittlebait brooded. 'Pretty big mouthful,' he said. 'Four spades.'

Sybil frowned and bid five diamonds.

'Double,' said Squareless.

'Seven spades,' said Mr. Whittlebait.

Sybil slapped down her hand. 'Really, Mr. Whittlebait,' she said, 'that's ridiculous.'

'Ssh,' said Squareless. 'The auction isn't over. I double.'

'Double check,' said Mr. Whittlebait. 'No, that ain't it. Redouble.'

Tim led a heart, properly, and Sybil spread her cards hopelessly. 'It's on your own head,' she growled. 'Not a spade in the hand.'

Mr. Whittlebait considered the dummy sadly. 'I ain't worried about the spades,' he said, 'but we sure are short on kings.'

'Mind if I stand behind him?' Sybil asked Squareless.

'All right,' said Squareless. 'But no coaching.'

Sybil walked around the table and looked at the cards which Mr. Whittlebait held in trembling fingers. The spades were beautiful, certainly, eight of them to four top honors, and he had the king of clubs, once guarded. She couldn't really blame him for having bid his grand slam, but he had the jack and a small heart and one small diamond. Unless the heart finesse worked, there wasn't a chance that she could see.

Mr. Whittlebait sighed deeply and played the ace of hearts from the board.

'Oh,' Sybil couldn't help exclaiming, 'the finesse was our only hope!'

'Dangnation,' said Mr. Whittlebait. He led out his ace and king of clubs.

'Many a man is walking the streets of London, Mr. Whittlebait,' murmured Sybil, 'because he failed to lead trumps.'

'Is that why many a girl walks the streets of London?' asked Tim.

'No coaching,' grumbled Squareless. 'And no badinage, either.'

'Well,' said Mr. Whittlebait, shaking his head, 'reckon all I can do now is lead these here spades and hope somebody makes a mistake.' He led the ace and both of the others followed.

'There won't be any mistakes,' said Squareless.

'Maybe not,' said Mr. Whittlebait. 'I'll bet I can make the danged thing anyhow. Bet you five bucks.'

'Mr. Whittlebait!' protested Sybil.

'I wouldn't take your money,' said Squareless, 'but I'll put up five dollars against you trimming my rosebushes.'

'Taken,' said Mr. Whittlebait.

'Mind if I peek at your hand?' Sybil asked Squareless. He shrugged and she peeked. He had both kings over dummy's hearts and diamonds. 'I can't watch,' said Sybil and walked to the window. She stared at the rain. Mr. Whittlebait went on leading spades and shaking his head.

Mrs. Barrelforth appeared in the doorway. 'I say, Mrs. Ludlow,' she called across the room, 'somebody's been sending you mash notes.'

Squareless looked up angrily. 'Wait till after the hand,' he snapped.

Mr. Whittlebait looked around in sorrowful reproof. Mrs. Barrelforth was waving a folded sheet of lined notepaper, then, seeing the disapproving eyes at the table, she stuck it in the pocket of her tweeds.

Sybil crossed the room quickly. 'What is it?' she asked, softly so as not to disturb the players.

'Blowed if I know,' said Mrs. Barrelforth. 'Take a look.'

Tim looked up from his cards and, even across the room, saw Sybil's hands tremble as she read. The color drained from her face.

'What is it, dear?' he asked.

'For God's sake,' interrupted Squareless, 'let's finish the hand and everybody can yammer all they want to.'

'It's nothing,' said Sybil. Her voice was shaky. 'It's a joke of some sort.'

'Fine time for a joke,' said Squareless. 'Play a card, Ludlow.'

'It's your play,' said Tim.

'Oh,' said Squareless. He looked at his hand. Mr. Whittlebait had just discarded the queen of hearts from dummy on his last spade, leaving the ace and queen of diamonds.

'Sybil,' said Tim, 'are you sure — '

'Shut up,' said Squareless. He pulled the king of hearts out of his hand, then put it back and looked peculiarly at Mr. Whittlebait. 'There's something rotten in the state of Denmark,' he said.

'There certainly is,' said Mrs. Barrelforth.

'Quiet!' roared Squareless. He played the king of hearts.

Meekly, Mr. Whittlebait led the good jack. Squareless threw down his cards with a throaty yelp and reached for his wallet. 'Whittlebait,' he demanded, slapping a five-dollar bill on the table, 'was that just luck?'

Mr. Whittlebait's watery eyes blinked at him. 'Well, it was and it wasn't,' he said. 'I figured if I kept on leadin' them spades, somebody was bound to slip up.'

'Nobody slipped up,' said Squareless. 'What you have just pulled off was a

176

perfect Vienna coup.'

'A what?' asked Mr. Whittlebait.

'A Vienna coup. Establishment of an honor in your opponent's hand so you can squeeze him later on. And I've never heard of it happening by luck.'

'Guess you have now,' said Mr. Whittlebait.

'I wonder,' said Squareless.

Mr. Whittlebait's walrus mustache quivered. 'Mr. Squareless,' he said in a hurt voice, 'if I've done something wrong, it was out of ignorance. But I'd a sight rather not take your money.'

Squareless stared at him, then a slow grin spread over his face, which had grown quite red. 'It's your money, all right,' he said. 'And when you get back to the store, you can tell the boys you pulled a Vienna coup against the best bridge player in — in Merry Point,' he finished with wry lameness.

'One of the best bridge players in Merry Point,' said Sybil. She was still pale, but her voice was calm, even gay.

'All right,' said Squareless, 'one of the best.' He stood up and stretched. 'Thank you, Lady Sybil, for a lively afternoon. I've enjoyed it, even if I didn't sound like it.' He started toward the door, then paused. 'What was all this about mash notes?'

'Nothing,' said Sybil. 'Nothing at all.'

'Then why all the fuss?' demanded Squareless. 'Even Garcia would have waited with a Vienna coup going on.'

He nodded shortly around the room and went out. Mr. Whittlebait made his humble adieux and followed him.

Tim absently picked up the cards and watched Sybil. Mrs. Barrelforth was watching her, too. Sybil crossed the room and poured herself a drink. 'Anybody else?' she asked.

'Please,' said Mrs. Barrelforth.

'Tim?'

'I'd like to see that note first,' said Tim.

Sybil looked at him hesitantly, biting her lip.

'I've already read it,' said Mrs. Barrelforth cheerfully.

'Oh,' said Sybil. She gave a nervous little laugh and tossed the crumpled sheet of paper onto the card table. Tim picked it up and read: 'Mrs. Ludlow. If you are smart you will not say anything at the inquest tomorrow about recognizing the body on the pier. You won't say anything about getting this good advice, either.'

17

Not a Fit Night

'What's it all about, anyway?' asked Mrs. Barrelforth. 'It sounds to me like a case for the Association.'

'As what isn't?' murmured Sybil.

'Where did you find the note, Mrs. Barrelforth?' asked Tim.

'In what I presume is the guest room,' said Mrs. Barrelforth. 'It was pinned to the pincushion on the dressing table. Therefore, it must have been left by someone who thought that was your bedroom. Therefore, it must have been someone unfamiliar with the house.'

'Not necessarily,' said Sybil. 'I usually use that room as my dressing room.'

'Oh,' said Mrs. Barrelforth. 'Didn't realize I was putting you out. Pity. In that case, we'll have to reverse our field. The note must have been left by someone who was familiar with the house but didn't know I was going to spend the night. Logical, what?'

'Also,' said Tim, 'it was apparently left by someone who didn't want me to find it.'

'Logical, logical,' agreed Mrs. Barrelforth. 'Already the web of logic begins to close in on the culprit. Next comes opportunity. Who had the opportunity to leave the note between the time when you, my dear, so kindly prepared the room for me and the time when I inadvertently discovered it?'

'I'm trying to think,' said Sybil. 'It's possible that the note was there when I got the room ready.'

'Hardly,' said Mrs. Barrelforth with assurance. 'You were about to rejoin your guests, so you must have had a look in the mirror before you came downstairs. In which event, you couldn't have missed the note.'

Sybil smiled. 'Quite right. I did look in the mirror, and I'm sure there was no note then.'

'That narrows it down,' said Mrs. Barrelforth. 'Slowly the web closes in.

Except that webs don't close in, do they? No matter. Is there just the one staircase?'

'There's a back staircase from the kitchen.'

'Aha,' said Mrs. Barrelforth. 'Was the kitchen door locked?'

'No,' said Sybil. 'I left it open so people could go to the privy.'

'B-r-r-r,' said Mrs. Barrelforth with a shiver. 'Don't remind me of that privy.'

'It's an item, though,' said Tim. 'Because everybody in the room made at least one trip outdoors during the afternoon. Ruling out the three of us, either Squareless or Whittlebait could easily have slipped up the back stairs and left the note.'

'Why rule out the three of us?' asked Mrs. Barrelforth. 'How do I know, Ludlow, that you didn't write this note to your wife for some sinister reason of your own? How do I know Mrs. Ludlow didn't write it to herself?'

'And how do we know,' asked Sybil, 'that you didn't write it and produce it in order to spoil poor Mr. Whittlebait's grand slam?'

'As a matter of fact,' said Mrs. Barrelforth calmly, 'I did produce it with malice aforethought. I hoped it would bring a reaction that would point to the perpetrator.'

'Did it?' asked Tim.

Mrs. Barrelforth pursed her lips. 'It certainly rattled your Mr. Squareless,' she said.

Sybil laughed, a merry and unforced laugh. 'Mrs. Barrelforth,' she said, 'you're not a bridge player. If you were, you'd realize that in the middle of a redoubled grand slam, depending on a Vienna coup, you'd have got the same reaction if you'd produced a plate of fudge or a live cobra.'

'Humph,' said Mrs. Barrelforth. 'Let's get back to fundamentals. Whose body on what pier at what inquest is the blasted note talking about?'

'I don't think we need go into it,' said Sybil.

'Dash it,' said Mrs. Barrelforth, 'how is the Association going to help you if we don't go into it?'

'I wasn't aware of having asked for the Association's help,' said Sybil.

Mrs. Barrelforth looked at the ceiling. 'I hate to bring up the subject of the roof over your heads,' she murmured, 'but — '

Sybil smiled wearily. 'There was a suicide,' she said. 'An old pine woods man shot himself on the pier. Tim and I happened to find his body. That's all.'

'Did you recognize him?'

'Of course not.'

'Why does the writer of this note think you did?'

'I haven't the faintest idea.'

'Humph,' said Mrs. Barrelforth again.

'Thinking the whole thing over,' said Sybil, and Tim felt the brittleness in her voice again, 'the note is undoubtedly the pine woods community's way of letting us know it doesn't want us poking into its affairs. Mr. Whittlebait was probably delegated to deliver it.'

'It doesn't sound like pine woods jargon,' said Mrs. Barrelforth.

'They go to the movies,' said Sybil.

'So do I,' said Mrs. Barrelforth, 'and my movie-trained mind doesn't think your explanation is worth two pins. You don't either. One of the first things we teach our brides is to confide in the Association. We're mothers to others, so why not to you?'

'Is that your slogan?' asked Sybil.

'It will be,' said Mrs. Barrelforth. 'I just made it up.'

She stalked exasperatedly across the room. Suddenly Tim and Sybil heard a horrified boom of 'Good God!' They both turned.

'We're out of Scotch,' said Mrs. Barrelforth. She stared at Tim with anxious eyes. 'Is there — by any chance —'

'Mrs. Barrelforth,' said Tim, 'how do you stand on rum?'

The President of the New Jersey chapter beamed and said, 'Like fifteen men on the dead man's chest.'

★ ★ ★

Tim woke in darkness. What had awakened him? It might have been the wind, still hurling its noisy weight against the house, or the rain still beating on the windows, but it seemed to him that something else, something more specific, had pierced his sleep. He realized slowly that Sybil was not beside him, and a moment later he heard, or thought he heard, the sound that must have awakened him. It was scarcely distinguishable from the rowdy elements, but he was almost sure, as he sat up in bed and strained to listen, that somebody was hammering at the front door and that a voice was crying out against the wind and rain and pounding ocean.

He slipped out of bed and peered into the dark hall. Simultaneously another door opened a few feet away and a voice, reassuringly familiar, said, 'That you, Ludlow? Thought I heard somebody at the door.'

'So did I, Mrs. Barrelforth,' said Tim. Her large, comfortable presence, voluminous in the gray Army bathrobe he had lent her, was extremely welcome just then. He flipped the switch at the head of the stairs, which controlled the light in the hallway below. 'I'll take a look,' he said.

As he padded down the stairs, with Mrs. Barrelforth behind him, there was a noise in the kitchen, then Sybil appeared in the dining room doorway. She was wearing her tweed coat over pajamas, the trousers of which clung damply to her ankles. Her face and hair were glistening wet. 'Hello,' she said. 'Did I wake everybody up?'

'Where've you been?' asked Tim.

'Indelicate question. No pleasure jaunt, either, on a night like this.'

As she spoke, the hammering at the front door came again, unmistakable now, accompanied by a human cry that rose, harsh and desperate, above the wind. Sybil whirled and exclaimed, 'My God! What's that?'

Tim walked swiftly to the door and drew back the heavy bolt. He opened it carefully, bracing himself to prevent the wind from sending it flying. A tall, angular, bedraggled figure wrapped in a dark cloak lurched in and staggered against the coat stand, clutching at it for support.

Sybil cried, 'It's Mr. Squareless's housekeeper!'

The woman lifted her gaunt face — which was white as death, the skin strained tight across the stony features. 'Mr. Squareless has been shot,' she said. 'You'd better come.'

18

For Man or Beast

Tim pulled his trenchcoat over his pajamas. The Luger and the flashlight, he was glad to note, were still in the pockets. He fetched the car and drove up under the porte-cochere, where the three women were waiting. Clutching their hasty wraps over their nightclothes, they looked like refugees from flood or fire. They climbed into the car and Tim drove off through the wind-whipped, sodden dunes.

Sybil sat beside Tim while Mrs. Barrelforth sat in back beside the stiff, unyielding figure of the housekeeper. Tim could see the latter's grim white face in the windshield mirror. She seemed to be holding herself in control with tight-lipped effort, but Mrs. Barrelforth managed, with gentle prodding, to get a few halting sentences out of her.

She had been awakened, she said, by a

loud noise of some sort and, while she was collecting her wits, she heard it again. The report of a gun, it sounded like, close to the house but not inside. She went downstairs from her second-floor bedroom to see if everything was all right. There was light under the door to Squareless's den, but that wasn't unusual. She knocked and, when there was no reply, pushed the door open. Squareless was slumped sideways in his big easy chair by the fire and, at first, she thought he had merely fallen asleep. Then, in the pool of light cast by the room's lone lamp, she saw that blood was running down his face, apparently from a wound in his head. His eyes were closed but when she approached and touched his shoulder, they had opened. 'Better get help,' he was able to say, then his eyes closed again. She had paused to soak a cold towel, which she laid over the wound. Then she had hurried off into the night.

'There's no phone, I take it,' said Mrs. Barrelforth.

The housekeeper shook her head.

'In that case,' said Mrs. Barrelforth, as Tim swung the car into the Squareless driveway, 'you'd better leave Mrs. Ludlow and myself to apply what first aid we can while you high-tail it for the nearest doctor.'

'I picked up a bit of nursing in the ATS,' said Sybil.

'I'm no slouch as a nurse myself,' said Mrs. Barrelforth.

'That's all very well,' said Tim, 'but I'm not going to leave three women alone to deal with any murderers who may be around.'

'We can discuss that after we survey the situation,' said Mrs. Barrelforth.

The gate in the stone wall stood open and the car slid to a stop on the wet gravel in from of the tall, dark house. At the side, where the windows of Squareless's den curved out, faint yellow light was visible between the curtains.

'You'd better go first,' Sybil said to the housekeeper, 'in case Goethe doesn't recognize us.'

'I don't know where Goethe is,' said the housekeeper woodenly. 'I called him but he didn't come.'

They followed the angular figure along the flagstones, through the rain, and into the house. She switched on a single bare light in the hallway, then, putting her finger to her lips as if from force of habit, tapped on the master's door. From within came a weak and indistinct groan. 'It's Julia,' she said, apparently interpreting the groan as a query, and opened the door.

Squareless sat under the lamp's cone of light. The rest of the room, the sweeping curtains, the mounted heads, the rows of books, melted into shadow. Evidently he had tried to move since the housekeeper left him. He was no longer slumped sideways, but looked as if he had tried to sit up and then had slid down in the chair. One hand clutched at the leather arm, stubby fingers spread, while the other was pressed to the wet white towel, coiled like a turban around his head. Against the whiteness, the dark red splotch looked almost like an embroidered flower between the short fingers. The blood on his face, which was almost as white as the towel but grayer, looked dry. His eyes were open and looking at them. His lips moved a little, but there was no sound.

Mrs. Barrelforth walked across the soft carpet to his side. 'Let's have a look,' she said, her voice cool and professional. Squareless let his hand fall and she lifted the towel. Then she put it back, holding it there, and turned to the housekeeper.

'I'll need a lot of things,' she said. 'Some blankets and a pillow to begin with. Then a razor, some adhesive tape, scissors, hot water, and some kind of bandages. Strips of cloth will do.'

From between Squareless's clenched teeth came two words: 'And brandy.'

'By all means,' said Mrs. Barrelforth. 'We could all use some.'

The housekeeper nodded and went out.

'You, Ludlow,' Mrs. Barrelforth went on, 'get going for a doctor.'

Squareless heaved himself up in his chair. His voice came in painful jerks. 'No! No doctor.' Tim hesitated at the door. Again Squareless spoke, his voice labored but commanding. 'No doctor. I forbid it.'

Tim looked at Mrs. Barrelforth. She

stared down at Squareless, then shrugged. 'All right,' she said. 'As far as I can tell, it's only a scalp crease. Even so — well — '

She was silent, holding the towel to Squareless's head. He subsided in the chair, breathing hard. The housekeeper came back with the blankets and pillow and went out again.

'Give us a lift, Ludlow,' said Mrs. Barrelforth.

They spread one blanket on the floor in front of the fireplace, pushing hassocks and taborets aside, and slid Squareless onto the blanket, his head resting on the pillow. He made grumbling noises but didn't protest otherwise.

'You've got to lie down and keep warm,' said Mrs. Barrelforth.

The housekeeper came back with the rest of the articles requested except bandages. 'I brought a sheet,' she said.

'Good,' said Mrs. Barrelforth. 'Tear it into strips, will you, you and Mrs. Ludlow.'

She bathed the wound, which, Tim saw now, was just above Squareless's right ear. 'Razor,' she said with a surgeon's briskness. The housekeeper handed her a straight razor and she deftly shaved the hair around the wound. 'Adhesive. Scissors. Matches.' She cut a strip of adhesive tape and ran the flame of a match along it, then pressed it firmly to the naked little oval in the grizzled hair. 'Bandages.' Sybil handed her strips of cloth and Mrs. Barrelforth wound them around and over Squareless's scalp until she had achieved a neat white-cap effect. Then she sighed complacently and looked up. 'Now,' she said, 'brandy.'

The housekeeper handed her a decanter and a balloon-shaped glass. 'Get a tumbler,' said Mrs. Barrelforth sharply. 'He doesn't want to sniff the bouquet. Fetch several while you're about it.'

A faint grin crossed Squareless's drained face.

'I'd feel better if this thing had a couple of stitches in it,' Mrs. Barrelforth said to Tim. 'However, there's a limit even to what the Association can do, and if our friend doesn't want a doctor, that's his privilege.'

Squareless gave a gratified grunt.

'Although,' Mrs. Barrelforth added, 'an apple a day isn't much help when you're shot. Ah, here we are.' She poured a stiff hooker of brandy into the tumbler the housekeeper handed her and lifted Squareless's head while she held the glass to his lips. Squareless smacked them.

'My best brandy,' he murmured. 'Eighty years old.' From his weak voice it wasn't clear whether he was pleased or annoyed.

'Delighted to hear it,' said Mrs. Barrelforth, filling glasses with ease and aplomb for Sybil, Tim, and herself. She glanced hesitantly at the housekeeper.

'No, thank you,' said the housekeeper coldly.

'Here's luck,' said Mrs. Barrelforth to Squareless. 'And, believe me, you've had plenty tonight. An eighth of an inch to the left and — well, here's luck.'

She drank, and so did the others. Tim could feel the bracing warmth spread all through him. It was a good feeling, and his brain seemed to grow clear along with it.

'If we're not going to call a doctor,' he

said, 'I presume the next step is to notify the police.'

An angry rumble came from Squareless and he tried to lift his head. 'Damn it, sir,' he gritted, 'there is no need to involve the law.' Then his head fell back.

'Easy,' warned Mrs. Barrelforth.

Tim stared around, bewildered. He had been brought up to call the police in certain given circumstances and he had always assumed other people did the same. Sybil's eyes met his impassively.

'I give up,' said Tim. 'What is the next step?'

'A little more brandy, if you're asking me,' said Mrs. Barrelforth cheerfully. 'And if Mr. Squareless feels up to it, perhaps he'll tell us in a few words what happened.'

Squareless's chest heaved irritably. 'If you *must* know,' he said, articulating with difficulty, 'I was cleaning one of my guns. As you see, I have a great many. Damned thing went off, that's all.'

'And you thoughtfully put it back?' said Mrs. Barrelforth.

'I was just putting it back as it went off.'

'I see,' said Mrs. Barrelforth. She waited a moment, then casually, glass in hand, strolled across the room to the curving windows. She glanced back at Squareless's easy chair and seemed to be calculating briefly, then passed her hand over the panes between two of the half-drawn curtains. She smiled to herself and walked back to the fireplace.

'Strange,' she said idly, 'there's a little round hole in one of the windows. Hail, perhaps.'

Again Squareless mumbled and again his head thrust itself up from the pillow. 'By God,' he blurted in feeble rage, 'I've had enough of you poking about. I've told you what happened. I'm grateful for your help. Now leave me alone. D'you hear me? Leave me alone!'

A mottled pink had suffused his face and his eyes glared balefully. Then his head fell back on the pillow once more, and his eyelids slowly shut. His breathing, after a convulsive jerk or two, became regular and peaceful. He began to snore.

'Looks like a reasonably healthy sleep,' said Mrs. Barrelforth. 'He's lost a good bit of blood but he's still got enough to color up with. A good sign. Still, somebody had better stay with him, just in case.'

'I'll be here,' said the housekeeper.

'What would you do in the event of a hemorrhage?' asked Mrs. Barrelforth. The housekeeper was silent.

'How about you?' Mrs. Barrelforth asked Sybil.

'I know what to do,' said Sybil quietly. 'I'll stay.'

'Good girl,' said Mrs. Barrelforth.

'You don't stay without me,' said Tim.

'Nonsense,' said Sybil. 'I'll be quite all right.'

'Is there any reason to think,' asked Tim, 'that Mr. Squareless's gun may not go off again?'

'I think it most unlikely,' said Sybil.

'Okay,' said Tim. Sybil glanced at him suspiciously and he thought perhaps he had yielded too suddenly. But she didn't say anything more.

The housekeeper walked to the front door with Tim and Mrs. Barrelforth. It was still raining, but the wind had died down and the faint, gray tinge of false dawn appeared beyond the quietly breathing ocean.

'Well — ' Mrs. Barrelforth began, but the housekeeper interrupted her.

'I think Mr. Ludlow's right,' she said. 'We should call the police.'

'Thank God somebody else thinks so,' said Tim. 'What about it, Mrs. B.?'

'The victim seems rather strongly opposed to it.'

'There's such a thing as carrying a passion for privacy too far,' said Tim.

'It's more than that,' said Mrs. Barrelforth. 'Hasn't it occurred to you, Ludlow, that our friend Squareless knows, or thinks he knows, who shot him?'

Tim stared at her. Then he said slowly, 'You may have something there.'

'Of course I have,' said Mrs. Barrelforth, 'but I'm not sure what. I'm a stranger here myself. A very sleepy stranger, I might add. Let's go.'

'You can drive, can't you?' asked Tim.

'Yes. Why?'

'I think I'll stick around a while.' He glanced into the gray darkness and lowered his voice. 'Wait till we're in the car,' he said to the housekeeper, 'then switch off the hall light. I'll slip out and Mrs. Barrelforth can drive away.'

'A quixotic plan,' said Mrs. Barrelforth, 'but I suppose it'll make you feel better.'

'It will also make me feel better,' said the housekeeper. 'We are in the midst of evil. I am frightened.'

'Try a little brandy,' said Mrs. Barrelforth encouragingly. 'It'll change your whole outlook.'

'Among other things that worry me,' said the housekeeper, ignoring the suggestion, 'is what has happened to Goethe. It would be terrible if he attacked Mr. Ludlow.'

'Goethe?' repeated Mrs. Barrelforth. 'Ah, yes, you mentioned him. The watchdog, I take it.'

'Yes.'

'That,' said Mrs. Barrelforth, snapping her fingers softly, 'explains there having been two shots. I'm afraid your Goethe is past attacking anyone. Let's have your torch, Ludlow.'

She took Tim's flashlight and stepped through the doorway into the dripping rain. Sending a yellow circle ahead of her, she walked across the lawn, then suddenly stopped. 'Look,' she called.

Tim hurried to her side, through the wet grass that brushed his bare ankles. The housekeeper followed him. In the blob of light that silvered the rain lay a dark, furry shape. Four legs stuck stiffly out of it, so stiffly that they almost seemed to quiver. Tim could hear the housekeeper's short, horrified breaths.

'Poor old boy,' said Mrs. Barrelforth. She doused the flashlight and handed it back to Tim. 'Nothing to be done about it now. Let's be off.'

19

Three Guesses

The hall light went off and Tim crawled awkwardly past Mrs. Barrelforth's large knees and out of the unfastened door on her side of the car. She gave him a couple of seconds to reach the shelter of the stone wall, then sent the car forward with a crash of worn gears. Crouched in the shadows, Tim listened to the sound of the engine growing fainter and fainter among the dunes, and his spirits fell with it. Mrs. Barrelforth's departure made him realize how comforting her hearty presence had been, just as the evanescence of false dawn made it seem darker than ever. An advantage, no doubt, but a double-edged one.

He heard footsteps in the gravel driveway and jumped, then recognized the figure of the housekeeper coming to shut the gate. It closed with a crunch and he heard the rusty bolt pushed into place. Then the footsteps passed near him again and re-entered the house. The front door closed, and then there was silence everywhere except for the steady, oblivious drip of the rain.

Now that his vigil had actually begun, it seemed a more nebulous undertaking than it had when the brandy was hot in his throat. It was like the eternal vigilance of liberty — a commendable idea but hard to put into practice. At any rate, he had better be moving about, he decided, before his feet, squishing in soaked bedroom slippers, grew numb. He started sidling cautiously along the wall as well as he could among the bushes that hid its base. Their rustle as he pressed through them sounded so loud that he felt like General Braddock's redcoats crashing four abreast through the Pennsylvania forests to surprise the twig sensitive Indians.

He drew even with the corner of the house from which swelled the embrasure of Squareless's den. It was only a rounded outline now, no light showing, not even the glint of rain on the windows. Still, remembering where Mrs. Barrelforth had spotted the hole in the glass, he could more or less reconstruct what must have happened. The ground sloped away from the house, but a man standing close to the windows would have found their ledges roughly level with his chest. Between the parted curtains of the first window he would have had Squareless's easy chair directly in front of him and almost facing him, as Tim recalled its position. Chances were, he thought, that Squareless must have heard a noise and turned his head slightly just as the shot was fired.

But matters of this sort, he told himself irritably, were obviously matters for the police. Why the devil didn't anybody want to call the police? Did Squareless have something to hide? Why was Sybil so leery of the normal processes of law and order? That damned editorial crept into his mind again, and just then the end window opened.

Sybil's head and shoulders appeared, framed by a faint and ruddy light that evidently came from the coal fire. There was no reason to suppose, certainly, that she was doing anything more than taking a breath of air, and yet, in his tired brain, a queer little suspicion was taking shape. Was it conceivable that she was expecting someone? Was that why she had insisted on staying?

He tried to brush such thoughts aside by concentrating on how beautiful she was in the light that just tipped her features. Apparently she was resting her elbows on the sill, her chin cupped in her hands. Tim thought of that night when the bomb fell in St. James's Park, of her white face turned toward him in the moonlight.

Even as he watched her, she grew more distinct. The darkness was yielding to a thick, wet gray as the real dawn appeared like a pale patch above the rim of the ocean. Tim glanced toward the eastern horizon, and then he saw that he was not the only one who was watching Sybil.

The upper half of a man's body protruded from the bushes that apparently marked the end of the lawn and the beginning of dunes. He wasn't more than twenty yards away, but it was still too dark for Tim to see what he looked like. He seemed to have a hat on, and he was standing motionless, but more than that Tim couldn't tell.

Then Sybil closed the window and the glow of the fire vanished with her as, evidently, she let the curtain fall back into place. Tim's eyes moved quickly back to the fringe of bushes in time to see the intruder drop out of sight in the amorphous thicket.

Or was he, Tim, the intruder? Had he stumbled upon the carrying out of some prearranged signal? Sybil couldn't have seen the man, he was sure, but that wouldn't prevent the opening of the window from having been something agreed upon.

But why, by God, shouldn't the man himself answer these questions? The very thought, with its angry promise of satisfaction, turned into energy and he scuttled in a crouch along the wall till he reached the row of bushes. Edging among the brambly clumps toward the spot where the man had stood, he saw that immediately beyond them the ground fell steeply and sharply to the beach. It was almost like the white cliffs of Dover in miniature, a drop of perhaps fifteen feet but curving at the bottom into soft sand.

Cautiously he poked his head through the bushes and over the crumbly edge of the sudden descent. Grayness shrouded the beach, but its pale meeting with the dark inlet was clear enough, and he was able to make out a small and rickety wharf at which two rowboats seemed to be tied up. One, no doubt, was Squareless's dinghy.

Before he could wonder about the other one, something moved directly beneath him. He was lying flat on his stomach now and he slithered forward until he could look straight down. A man — it had to be the same man — was standing in the shelter of the little cliff, looking toward the sea, his back toward Tim.

Tim lifted himself on his hands, then to all fours, then to a crouch. He took the Luger out of his pocket, then slowly and laboriously he slipped off the trenchcoat. With the gun in his hand, he jumped.

His feet struck the sand with a splash,

but the rest of him hit the target. The man went over like a nine-pin, yelling as he did so, 'Mother of God!'

'You again, eh?' muttered Tim. He had landed astride the man's back and he jabbed his knees into the other's ribs and touched his head with the butt of the Luger. 'Keep still,' he said, 'or I'll cave your skull in.'

'You will, will you?' said a voice behind him, and something cold and metallic touched his own head.

Tim sat perfectly still. He was aware of terror, but objectively, as if he were watching himself from a distance. It seemed quite natural for him to say, 'Night fishing again, are you?'

'Yes,' said the voice behind him. 'We like to fish at night. But we don't like people butting in.'

'I'm not surprised,' said Tim.

'Why?'

'Three guesses.'

The cold metal was withdrawn. 'One, two, three,' said the man behind him, and those were the last words that Tim heard for a while. Afterward, he couldn't remember whether the blow on his head had actually hurt or not; all he remembered was the sudden blackness, a blaze of fireworks, and then nothing.

It was broad daylight when he opened his eyes, although even after a wholesome nap it would have been hard to recognize it as such in the heavy mist and drizzle. He was lying on his face in the sand and his first sensation was that his mouth was full of gritty stuff. His next was a dull, throbbing ache in the back of his head. He sat up and looked around. The beach, as far as he could see in the thickness, was deserted. Then, painfully, his eyes moved toward the little wharf and he saw that only one rowboat was tied up.

He got slowly to his feet, sending a stab through his head, and realized that he was cold, so cold that he was shaking all over. He sneezed twice and wondered how long he had been there. Not too long, judging by the pale light, but long enough to warrant immediate steps if he wasn't to get pneumonia.

He looked up doubtfully at the overhanging cliff, then further along he saw that from the wharf a narrow board-walk led to a flight of wooden stairs that hugged the wall. He paused to look around for the Luger, but naturally enough it wasn't in evidence. Then he made his way to the stairs and mounted to the lawn. It would have been a bleak enough expanse, wet and shaggy around the sagging brown house, even without the grim figure in the center of it: stiff-legged Goethe, fur as limp as a muskrat's.

He found his trenchcoat among the bushes — bayberry bushes he saw now — and its inner lining was dry. He stripped off his plastered pajamas and stood there for a moment before putting on the coat in order to wonder at the ways of a providence that landed an earnest young Fine Arts instructor naked on a strange lawn with a dead police dog for company.

Then he put on his trenchcoat, unlocked the front gate, and broke into a light trot for home and hot tub.

20

Three Photographs

Left alone in the big room, silent except for the hiss of the coals and Squareless's heavy breathing, Sybil first drew the red curtains tightly shut. Then she switched on a lamp that stood on the broad teakwood desk and turned off the other one, which had been shining directly down on Squareless's face, Hogarthian in its pallor under the cap of bandage.

She poured a little more brandy into her glass and carried it to the desk, behind which she settled herself for her vigil, even as Tim, less comfortably, was doing at the same time outside. The desk was still cluttered with papers — bills, accounts, letters, a catalogue of sporting books, a bridge hand clipped from a newspaper, all carelessly shoved together. There were a couple of books, *Burke's Peerage* and one about big-game hunting

212

in Kenya. Neither struck her as exactly fascinating, and she had no mind for reading, anyway.

Then she saw something on the desk that hadn't been there at the time of her previous visit. It was a leather folder, richly embossed, designed to hold three photographs, triptych fashion. The center photograph was of a young woman with bare shoulders rising from cloudy white drapery. Dark hair piled on top of her head gave her an ethereal Burne-Jones sort of beauty. But she was fully as beautiful in the picture at the left which showed her in ankle-length skirt and white blouse, wearing a straw hat and holding a tennis racket. Beside her stood a broad-shouldered young man, also in a straw hat and carrying a racket, and wearing a striped blazer over white flannels. There was no mistaking his youthfully rugged face as the one which now lay upturned across the room in fire-lit chiaroscuro.

The third photograph was of a baby, perhaps a year old, sitting on a cushion. It was a glum and rather puny child, and such charms as it had were not enhanced by the picture's being a blurred enlargement of a snapshot. It didn't look much better, though, in the original snapshot which, yellow and faded, was stuck into one corner of the frame.

Sybil remembered, then, that Squareless had gone into the room ahead of her after reluctantly admitting her to the house the day before.

She stared at the three photographs for a bit, then realized that they were swimming together before her tired eyes. She shook her head, blinking hard, and took a sip of brandy. That was better, but only for a minute or so. Again her eyelids began to droop. She switched off the lamp and walked to the window, which she opened after pulling the curtain aside. For a while she leaned on her elbows on the sill, breathing in the cold, wet freshness. When her brain had cleared a little, she closed the window and went back to her seat at the desk.

The last thing she remembered before she finally fell asleep was thick, gray light pushing against the red curtains, sifting around and under them into the room. When she woke up with a guilty start, everything was suffused in a gloomy clarity: the lion's head over the fireplace, the guns and the swords, the patterned carpet, and Squareless himself.

He had got himself back into his easy chair and he was sitting there, a blanket over his knees, beefy hands on the arms of the chair, his purple smoking-jacket open, showing bloodstains on his white shirt. His eyes were looking at Sybil from under the grotesque cap.

'About time you were waking up,' he said.

His voice was firm and, even in the opaque light, she could see that he was looking better. Better than she, probably.

'What time is it?' she asked.

'Half-past eight.'

'A.m.?'

'Yes.'

'How do you feel?'

'Groggy. Any more questions?'

'No,' said Sybil, taken aback at his brusqueness. 'Not for the moment.'

'Then I'll ask you one. What the devil

are you doing here?'

'Looking after you.'

'My housekeeper looks after me.'

'Even when you've been shot?'

'Damn it, you speak as if I were shot as a regular thing.'

Sybil chuckled. 'You seem to be a great deal better, Mr. Squareless,' she said. 'Quite normal, in fact. In which case, there's no further reason for me to poach on your housekeeper's preserve.'

'Poach,' repeated Squareless. 'What does that remind me of? Ah, yes. Eggs. I suppose I must offer you some breakfast.'

'I could do with some coffee.'

'I dare say Julia will be bringing some in a few minutes. Meanwhile, there's an item or two I'd like to get straightened out.'

'All right.'

'Come a bit closer, will you? I'm too damned weak to shout across the room.'

Sybil smiled at his petulance and walked across to the fireplace where the remains of the fire were a cold pink-gray. She leaned against the mantelpiece. 'Well?' she said.

Squareless looked up at her, drawing together his thick eyebrows. His words came evenly. 'Why didn't you finish me off while you had the chance?'

Sybil stared. 'What do you mean?'

'You know what I mean. You had one crack at me and missed. Why didn't you have another go?'

'If this is a joke, I'm not in the mood.'

'It's not intended as a joke.'

'You may be quite sure, Mr. Squareless,' she said lightly, 'that I would never shoot a fourth at bridge in a time of scarcity.'

Squareless grinned twistedly. 'You might,' he said, 'given sufficient reason.'

'And what sufficient reason could I possibly have?'

'I can think of at least three reasons, if you want to know them.'

'I certainly do.'

'Hand me my pipe, will you? On that little table. Some damned busybody must have moved it last night.'

Sybil brought him the pipe and tobacco pouch and waited while he filled, tamped, and finally lit it with a deliberation intended, she suspected, to be maddening. She watched him with a cool smile.

'In the first place,' said Squareless, 'you know that I know you're a fake.'

'A fake? In what way?'

He jerked his head toward the red volume on the desk. 'You noticed *Burke's Peerage* when you were here yesterday. And you know damned well you're not in it.'

'I know nothing of the sort. Why should I look myself up in anybody's stud book? I know who I am.'

'Burke doesn't.'

'Neither did my husband until long after we were married. And then through inadvertence. Let me make it quite clear, Mr. Squareless, that I have never exploited my station. I despise titles. Since you have seen fit to bring the subject up, may I suggest that if our family is not listed in your Burke, it is because the earldom died with my father.'

'Lady Sybil,' said Squareless, lingering with irony on the words, 'you may be telling the truth. Or you may be wriggling out of a tight corner. May I suggest

— since we are suggesting — that you have another, and considerably stronger, reason for wishing me out of the way?'

'Because you rented us a house with defective plumbing?'

'Please,' said Squareless. 'Like you, I am in no mood for joking. I am referring to the fact that I, and I alone, saw you go through the pockets of the body on the pier.'

'You must have very sharp eyes.'

'I have.'

'And you think that because you have such sharp eyes, I wish you out of the way?'

'Don't you?'

Sybil managed an incredulous little laugh. 'Simply because you happened to see me looking for something that might identify an unfortunate suicide?'

'You didn't need anything to identify him,' he said. 'You knew from the first that it was the body of Sam Magruder.'

She had herself under control again. 'Amazing,' she said. 'Because I haven't the faintest notion who Sam Magruder is.'

'Sam Magruder,' said Squareless, 'is, or was, a gray-haired gentleman fond of cards. Too fond, perhaps. He was a friend of your father's, and you spent an interesting hour with him the night you arrived in this country.'

Sybil turned her face, white and yet relieved, on Squareless. 'How did you know?' she asked, letting her voice tremble all it wanted to.

'Sam Magruder was also a friend of mine. It's no great coincidence. He was a friend of many people who are fond of cards and travel. Such people were his living. And it's to his everlasting credit that he could still be a friend.'

'So my father thought,' said Sybil. She sat quickly on the hassock because her legs had suddenly gone watery. Her mouth was dry and for a moment she couldn't speak. Then she asked, 'Did he tell you he had seen me?'

Squareless nodded. 'He wired me.'

'Why?'

'Don't try to fit me into your scheme of things,' said Squareless, smiling faintly. 'Sam wanted my house for you, that was all. He knew I had an empty one.'

'God bless him,' said Sybil. 'But then, where do Mrs. Barrelforth and her war brides come in?'

'Sounds like St. Ursula and her Virgins,' said Squareless. 'I'm not quite clear on that part myself. Apparently, though, Sam knew about this bridal association and knew that it acted as a middleman, or middlewoman, in matters of this sort. All he told me was that if I was willing to make the house available, this Barrelforth woman would handle the details.'

'You fibbed to us about the house, then, didn't you?'

'Very slightly. Sam didn't want his connection mentioned.'

Sybil was silent. For a moment she thought she was going to cry, then she got herself in hand again. 'Why have you told me all these things?' she asked.

'It's a form of blackmail,' said Squareless.

She glanced up at him uncertainly. Squareless grinned.

'I'm trying to blackmail you,' he said,

'into playing ball with me. I asked you yesterday to confide in me. I'm asking you again now.'

Sybil's eyes looked past him. 'Why should I,' she asked, 'when you haven't confided in me?'

'I have to a damned large extent.' After the tenseness of the conversation, the note of irritation sounded familiar and comfortable.

'There are three photographs on your desk,' said Sybil, 'that you hid from me the last time I was here.'

Squareless scowled at her, chewing his lip. 'I'd have hid them again,' he said, 'if I hadn't been flat on my back.'

'Why?' She waited a moment, then said, 'Mrs. Barrelforth told Tim and me that you had — had lost your wife in the other house.'

'Confound that nosy woman!' exploded Squareless. 'What the devil business is it of hers? Or of yours either, for that matter.'

Sybil laid a hand on the blanket where it covered his knee. 'Wouldn't it help if you told me about it?' she asked softly.

'No,' said Squareless. 'It's an extremely painful subject.' He glared down at her. 'And don't look at me like a damnable psychiatrist either. My wife died in childbirth and that's that.' He clamped his teeth on his pipe.

'And the child?' asked Sybil.

Squareless looked at the bowl of his pipe for a while, as if it might have tea leaves in the bottom. Then he said shortly, 'I lost the child, too, a couple of years later. And at the time, God help me, I was glad. I hated that child. It was only when it was too late that I realized — that I'd been wrong.'

Sybil patted his knee.

'Stop patting me, you half-baked Florence Nightingale,' roared Squareless, as if ashamed of his momentary weakness. 'Why don't you do something useful? Find out why the coffee hasn't come.'

Sybil rose, but just then there was a tap on the door and Julia entered with a laden brass tray. The housekeeper's stern face was haggard with dark circles under red-rimmed eyes.

'You're late,' said Squareless.

Julia put down the tray without replying. 'Will there be anything else?' she asked.

'No.'

Julia inclined her head slightly and went out, closing the door with careful quiet.

Sybil poured coffee into the two big cups. 'Tell me about Julia,' she said.

'My God,' said Squareless, 'she keeps house for me. What more is there to tell?'

'A good deal, I imagine.'

'Well, there isn't.'

'Has she always been with you?'

'Yes.'

'Was she here when your wife — '

'Yes. She was in the room.'

'Did she hate the child, too?'

'Not that I'm aware of.'

'Why does she stay with you?'

'Why the devil shouldn't she?'

'It must be a pretty grim sort of life,' said Sybil.

'I don't see why.'

Sybil smiled wryly into her coffee cup. 'Is she fond of you?' she asked.

'It's never occurred to me to ask her.'

'Has it ever occurred to you that she might hate you?'

'No.' Squareless stared at her. 'What are you driving at, anyway?'

'You know, don't you?'

'Are you suggesting that Julia might have shot me?'

'Not exactly. I'm wondering if *you* think she might have.'

Squareless looked past her at the lion's glassy eyes and sucked noisily on his pipe. 'I thought it was one of you,' he said finally. 'I don't want to think about it any more. Is that brandy still around?'

Sybil brought him the almost-empty decanter. Squareless gave a little yelp. 'Great God!' he shouted. 'What did you people do with my best brandy? Fill water pistols?'

21

The Bare Facts

Julia returned to say that the lady from the other house was waiting outside.

'That must be Mrs. Barrelforth,' said Sybil. 'Shall I ask her in?'

'Judas, no!' said Squareless. 'Take her away.'

Sybil stood up. 'Goodbye, then,' she said. 'Sure you're all right?'

'Hell, yes.'

'Still don't want a doctor?'

'Hell, no.'

Sybil turned toward the door, then paused. 'You know,' she said, 'you're rude and ungrateful and pigheaded. Why do I like you so much?'

'Because I play bridge,' growled Squareless. 'Trot along.'

She followed Julia into the hall, realizing, in the mundane daylight, that she was still in pajamas, her feet in muddy pink mules.

Mrs. Barrelforth, on the other hand, sat at the wheel of Tim's car looking as fresh and robust as ever in her sensible tweeds. 'Had any breakfast?' she boomed as Sybil climbed in beside her. 'If not, I'll fix you some flapjacks. D'you like flapjacks?'

'I don't know.'

'It's one of the first things we teach our brides,' said Mrs. Barrelforth, 'how to make flapjacks.'

'I see,' said Sybil. 'Why didn't Tim come?'

'He wanted to, but I put him to bed. With a hot-water bottle.'

'Why, for goodness' sake?'

Mrs. Barrelforth, steering erectly through the dunes, glanced sideways at her. 'He didn't go home, you know. He hung about.'

'Oh?' said Sybil. 'Rather silly of him, wasn't it?'

'He had quite a time. Somebody conked him. He'll tell you about it.'

In a tired way, Sybil realized that she should be agog with curiosity. And yet her own emotions of the past half-hour, coming on top of a nerve-racking night, were more than enough for her muzzy brain to cope with. Perhaps Mrs. Barrelforth saw this, because she didn't speak again during the short ride.

When they got back to the house, Mrs. Barrelforth once more raised the subject of flapjacks.

'I think I'll climb straight into bed,' said Sybil. 'I'm pretty well done in.'

'Right-o,' said Mrs. Barrelforth. 'I'll wake you in time for the inquest.'

'Damn,' said Sybil. 'I'd forgotten about the inquest.'

She dropped her tweed coat on the stand and trailed wearily upstairs. The blinds were drawn in the bedroom and it felt stuffy. There was a strong smell of wintergreen and camphor. Unreasonably, she felt irritated that Tim, whatever he had done, should be the object of all this solicitude. Particularly as she herself felt the need of fresh air.

'Hullo,' said Tim from the bed.

'Hullo,' said Sybil listlessly. She sat on the edge of the bed and kicked off her mules.

'I couldn't sleep till you got here.'

'Why not?'

'Because I was worried about you.' He sat up and put his arms around her. For a brief moment she yielded, then she pushed him away.

'Let's go to sleep,' she said. 'Even if I felt romantic, this sickroom atmosphere wouldn't do.'

'Mrs. Barrelforth insisted,' said Tim sheepishly. 'Did she tell you what happened to me?'

'Uh huh.' Sybil yawned. 'More or less.'

Tim felt deflated. He waited for her to say something more, but she only slid under the covers and stretched out luxuriously with her back to him.

'You ought to feel the lump on my head,' said Tim.

'Ought I?' Her voice was drowsy.

'Yes. It's the wifely thing to do.' He reached for her hand and guided its indifferent limpness to his head. 'Feel it? A real goose egg.'

But Sybil was already asleep.

★ ★ ★

Tim was awakened by a knocking on the door. Mrs. Barrelforth's cheerful voice announced that it was after twelve o'clock.

229

'Everybody up for the inquest,' she added.

'Oh,' groaned Sybil, sitting up beside him, 'what a horrid way to start a day.'

'There's a silver lining,' called Mrs. Barrelforth through the door. 'Or a copper one, anyway. The plumber's come and gone. Everything works.'

'Thank God for that,' said Sybil. She got up and started for the bathroom.

'I'll have flapjacks ready,' went on Mrs. Barrelforth. 'Put on plenty of warm clothes, Ludlow.'

A golden stack was waiting on the dining room table's blue and white checked cloth when they came downstairs. Also three glasses of tomato juice and a steaming pot of coffee.

'You can't enjoy an inquest on an empty stomach,' said Mrs. Barrelforth.

'I suppose you'd like us to drop you at the station en route,' said Tim, settling himself at the table.

'Well, I'm in no great rush,' said Mrs. Barrelforth. 'I trust nobody will object if I attend the proceedings. Might be interesting. Especially in view of that advice you got yesterday.'

'Gracious,' said Sybil. 'I'd forgotten about that.'

'Had you?' murmured Mrs. Barrelforth. 'Who wants syrup?'

★ ★ ★

They drove to Bankville under a sky that had grown lighter but remained dull and ominous. The rain had dwindled to a fineness that was invisible except where it struck the windshield. The wind hovered sullenly in the pines. The town's main street looked drab with its parked cars and neon signs, the latter looking cheap and garish in the gloomy daylight

The room in the brick Borough Hall, where the inquest was to be held, was musty and bare and damp, typical of the rooms to which, for some reason, the processes of self-government are generally assigned, as distinct from the congenial and comfortable hotel suites where the same processes are frequently contravened.

The coroner, a middle-aged man with a bald head and a pince-nez, sat at a wooden table. The Police Chief and Dr. Medford, who looked solidly like a doctor, sat in straight-backed chairs on either side of him. The rest of the chairs in the room were of the folding, or funeral, variety and only about a third of them were filled. Half a dozen pine woods people, including the storekeeper and Mr. Whittlebait, huddled together near the back. They all wore collars and ties and looked uncomfortable.

Such other spectators as were present were a seedy lot and looked as if they were only waiting for the rain to stop. A couple of those little gray men who float about courthouses and town halls, performing vague functions, completed the assemblage.

The entrance of Tim, Sybil, and Mrs. Barrelforth created a stir, but once they were seated, the atmosphere of listless boredom returned as the hearing got under way. The Chief read his report, beginning with a visit from Mr. Timothy Ludlow of Merry Point, covering his efforts to obtain identification — including a hint that he'd like more cooperation from the pine woods in future — and ending with consignment of the body and responsibility for same to Dr. Medford.

'Identifying witnesses,' said the coroner.

The Chief beckoned to two of the pine woods men, one the storekeeper, and they stood up in turn and each said much the same thing: that they had known the deceased by sight, that he lived in the woods back of Merry Point, and that, as far as they knew, he had no family.

'Doesn't anybody know his name?' asked the coroner.

'Apparently not,' said the Chief.

The coroner looked mildly annoyed and wrote something on a pad in front of him.

Tim watched Sybil from the corner of his eye. Her face, still slightly drawn after the night's strain, was composed but her fingers were twisted tightly together. Was the writer of the note in the courtroom?

'Let's have your report, Doc,' said the coroner.

Dr. Medford cleared his throat. Death had been caused by a bullet that had entered the right temple at such and such a point and embedded itself in the brain. It had been fired from close range, not more than six inches judging from burns and powder stains. The location of the wound and position of the body neither confirmed nor precluded the shot having been fired by the deceased. Rigor mortis had set in some time before he had reached the scene, and death had taken place six to twelve hours before. 'Can I go now?' he asked after he finished. 'I've got a baby due.'

'Run along, Doc,' said the coroner. 'Let's see, now. The folks that found the body — they here?'

He knew perfectly well they were, and he peered over his pince-nez at Sybil. 'You're the lady who saw it first, eh? Got anything to add to what the Chief told us?'

'Nothing of any importance,' said Sybil calmly.

A rustle of interest ran through the drowsy room. Feet scuffed and heads turned. For a moment Tim thought it was because she had been expected to say something else, then he decided it was merely the unfamiliar clipped accent. Certainly her clear voice freshened the proceedings.

'How about you, Mr. Ludlow?' asked the coroner. 'Anything to add?'

'I guess not,' said Tim.

'You guess not?' repeated the coroner with school-masterish reproof. 'Either you do or you don't, son.'

Tim flushed. 'I don't,' he said.

The coroner turned again to Sybil. 'You were walking on the beach and you see this fellow on the pier, is that it?'

'That's it,' said Sybil.

'How could you tell he was dead?'

'I couldn't. But I thought there must be something wrong with him. He didn't move or change his expression.'

'And you figured he ought to have taken more notice of a good-looking gal, eh?' The coroner chuckled and winked at the Chief.

'Yes,' said Sybil coolly. 'Particularly as I hadn't any clothes on.'

A delighted gasp rippled over the gathering, followed by sporadic titters.

Tim shifted uncomfortably in his seat and felt his face getting red. The reporter for the local paper sat up straight for the first time that morning. He was an A.P. string man and he sensed a couple of bucks' worth of space.

'Do tell,' said the coroner, looking happily shocked. 'Where were your clothes? Hanging on a hickory limb, I suppose.'

Everybody laughed, including Tim, who didn't want to act the outraged husband. The coroner beamed around.

'In a manner of speaking,' said Sybil, smiling impishly. 'I'd gone out for a dip.'

'That a habit of yours?' asked the coroner.

Before Sybil could answer, the Police Chief rolled jovially to his feet. 'I object,' he shouted. 'If the young lady says it is, half the town'll be hangin' around that beach and the other half'll be pesterin' me to do somethin' about it!'

The room broke into laughter. When order was finally restored and attention brought back to the subject of the hearing, the verdict of suicide was accepted as an anti-climactic matter of course.

22

Girl Friday

The Ludlows and Mrs. Barrelforth stood in the steaming vestibule of the Borough Hall, along with most of the others who had attended the inquest, and looked at the rain falling on the bare earth of the little yard in front. Two elm trees, with a few brown leaves still clinging to the black branches, quivered in the breeze. Now and then somebody would make up his mind and dart into the rain, to a parked car, to the lunch wagon down the street, to the neon-lit bar and grill across the way.

Mr. Whittlebait came up to pay his respects. 'Poorish weather,' he said, giving the bill of his cap a token tug.

'Very poorish,' said Sybil. 'What brings you here on a day like this?'

'I come mostly for the ride,' said Mr. Whittlebait. 'Kind of breaks the monotony, this time of year.'

'I can think of better ways to break it,' said Sybil.

'I'll bet you mean cards,' said Mr. Whittlebait. 'That's what I was gonna ask you — whether you figured on playin' this afternoon.'

'Afraid not,' said Sybil. 'Mr. Squareless isn't well.'

'That so?' Mr. Whittlebait looked surprised. 'He acted fit as a fiddle yesterday. Hope it wasn't losing his five bucks upset him.'

'I don't think so,' said Sybil with a smile.

'He must of been took sort of sudden.'

'Sort of.'

'Too bad,' said Mr. Whittlebait. He glanced toward the street where the pine woods contingent was waving at him from an old and shabby sedan. 'Guess I better be going, if I don't want to walk.' He tugged at his cap again and scuttled off through the rain.

Mrs. Barrelforth asked, 'Do you really think he delivered the mysterious warning?'

'This is no place to discuss it,' said Sybil.

'It's no place to linger, either,' said Mrs. Barrelforth, shivering. 'Especially with a train to catch.'

Tim went for the car and they drove to the station. The wet, windy platform was bare, and the waiting room was crowded and stuffy. A whistle sounded in the distance as Mrs. Barrelforth went to the ticket window, and a moment later the nearby crossing gates banged down. Mrs. Barrelforth called to Tim, 'Have you got three pennies? Otherwise I'll have to break a bill.'

Tim walked over to her, holding his loose change in his hand and looking for pennies. Mrs. Barrelforth leaned toward him and whispered, 'Don't worry if that note's missing when you get home. I've got it. Have faith in the Association.' Then she calmly bought her ticket as the train pulled in.

People were hurrying across the platform. Mrs. Barrelforth rushed up to Sybil and said, 'I'll keep in touch with you, my dear. And if you must find any more bodies, try to be more suitably dressed. Chin up, and cheerio!'

She sailed out of the waiting room with a majestic confidence that no train would dare leave without the President of the New Jersey chapter. Tim and Sybil followed in time to see her swing nimbly aboard just as it started to move. She stood at the top of the steps, waving.

'I like that woman,' said Sybil, 'but there's something fishy about her. Deucedly fishy.'

'On the contrary,' said Tim, 'she strikes me as the least fishy person I've been associating with lately.'

'Including me?'

'Definitely.'

Sybil raised her eyebrows and clucked. 'Speaking of things being fishy,' she said, 'I'd better lay in something for dinner while we're here.'

'We'd better lay in some whisky, too,' said Tim, 'if Mrs. Barrelforth's going to keep in touch with us.'

Rain still slanted across the gray countryside, and the dismal light of afternoon had begun to show signs of fading when they dumped their bags and parcels into the car. They drove out of town and entered the murky pine woods.

They had scarcely spoken during the shopping expedition and they remained silent now — a silence that grew strained and unnatural in the gloom of the interlaced trees. Tim broke it suddenly.

'Why the hell,' he asked, 'did you have to tell the whole courtroom you didn't have any clothes on?'

Sybil shrugged. 'It brightened the proceedings, didn't it?'

'I dare say it did. I dare say it also convinced a lot of people that I've married a trollop.'

'Do you think you have? Married a trollop?'

'I don't know,' said Tim. 'I don't know what I've married.'

Unexpectedly he jammed on the brakes, jolting Sybil forward. 'Oy,' she exclaimed, 'don't do things like that.'

Tim didn't answer. He stared at her with brooding eyes. 'What have I married, anyway?' he asked.

'What are you stopping for?'

'Because I can't drive and look you in the eye.'

'Why look me in the eye?'

'Sybil,' he said, and his voice was harsh, 'what did you marry me for?'

'The customary thing.'

'I'm not sure what the 'customary thing' is in your circles.'

'Really!' exclaimed Sybil. 'Stop acting like an idiot, Tim.'

'I'm not. I may be acting like a heavy husband, but nobody would blame me for that.'

'I would.'

'If you married me as a dodge to get into this country, I want to know. Right now.'

'I married you because I loved you. But I don't love you when you talk like this.'

'A woman who loved a man,' said Tim, 'would have shown a little interest, I should have thought, to hear he'd been slugged and damned near killed.'

'I tried to show an interest. I was worn out.'

'Would you have shown more interest if I'd mentioned the fact I saw you signaling out the window?'

'Me? Signaling? Are you mad?'

'It was hardly a coincidence that someone was waiting in Squareless's bayberry for a window to open and close.'

'Perhaps you think it was a lovers' rendezvous.'

'I wouldn't know. There usually is a lover in the offing, isn't there, when people marry for ulterior motives?'

Sybil's face was white in the car's dusky interior, and her breast heaved. Then she spoke very quietly: 'You don't know what you're saying, Tim. Please, I'd like to go home.'

'Back to Blighty?'

'Don't, Tim. You're not yourself.'

'Not by choice,' said Tim bitterly. He slammed the car into gear.

★ ★ ★

In the dying light, the house on the point looked empty and desolate as they rattled across the bridge and turned into the driveway. A couple of seagulls flapped lazily past it like birds of evil omen. Tim felt as Hansel might have if he'd had a quarrel with Gretel just before they met the witch.

Then, as they emerged from the dunes with the sound of the ocean loud in their ears, the whole bleak mood was shattered by the vehicle that stood under the porte-cochere. It was a snappy red convertible. Its occupant, Tim discovered after parking behind it and getting out for a look, was exactly what the coupé called for — a vivid redhead who happened to be sound asleep stretched out on the front seat.

Tim reached through the half-open window and tapped her shoulder. She wiggled drowsily, blinked, started to yawn, then suddenly sat up straight and stared at him with wide blue eyes. 'I do declare,' she said with a trace of a southern accent, 'I must have fallen asleep.'

She looked at Tim with amused wonder, and her extremely red lips parted in a smile. She was a very pretty girl, no doubt of that, but a second glance suggested that she wasn't quite as young or as dewy as the wide eyes and naive voice would have indicated.

Sybil had come up behind Tim. 'Who is it?' she asked.

'Don't know yet,' said Tim.

The girl took a look at Sybil and pulled down her skirt which, up to that point, she had only patted at in a desultory way. 'You all must be Mr. and Mrs. Ludlow,' she said. 'I'm Millie Marsden. Girl Friday for Ruth Royce Rollick.'

'What for who?' asked Sybil.

'Girl Friday,' repeated the redhead, enunciating distinctly, 'for Ruth Royce Rollick. You all must know who Ruth Royce Rollick is.'

'I don't,' said Sybil.

'I do,' said Tim. 'She runs some kind of radio program. Recipes and interviews and stuff. I've never actually heard her.'

'Good,' said Sybil. 'I was beginning to wonder.'

Tim didn't smile. He was still nursing his bitterness and he didn't propose to abandon it just because there was company. 'Well, what can we do for you, Miss — Martin was it?' he asked.

'Marsden. Millie Marsden. For a start,

you might ask me in and get me warm. I've been sitting here goodness knows how long.'

'I'm so sorry,' said Sybil. 'Do come in.'

The girl climbed stiffly out of the convertible and walked with Sybil up the porch steps. Tim, following, noticed that she was a bit shorter and plumper than he had supposed, but she wasn't unbecomingly short, and as for her plumpness, it was distributed in an interesting manner that became downright fascinating when she took off her reversible plaid coat to reveal a bright yellow sweater.

She sat gratefully in one of the easy chairs beside the fire and crossed her legs. 'Might as well come straight to the point,' she said. 'Ruth Royce is doing a show on war brides, and she'd like Mrs. Ludlow to appear on it.'

'A show?' queried Sybil.

'A program. She's rounded up half a dozen of the gals who landed the other day and she particularly wants you. For variety, you might say, you being the only title in the bunch.'

'Oh, dear,' said Sybil, 'that wretched

246

title again. You know, in twenty-odd years of living in England, I haven't been reminded as often of the jolly old title as I have in three days in the States.'

'Ain't it the truth,' said Millie. 'We eat 'em up.'

'What would I have to do on this program?' asked Sybil. 'Rattle my coronet?'

'It's very simple,' said Millie. 'Ruth Royce says something cute and then you say something cute. Anything you say in that accent will be cute. That's all.'

'Do I get paid?'

'Gosh, no!' Millie looked shocked. 'People give their back teeth to appear with Ruth Royce.'

'Oh,' said Sybil. 'Sorry. Anyway, it sounds like fun. When do the doings take place?'

'Tomorrow. Tomorrow afternoon at four. It's pretty short notice, but it's taken me quite a while to track you all down.'

'I'd rather like to have a go at it,' said Sybil. 'You wouldn't object, would you, Tim?'

'Wouldn't matter much if I did, would it?'

'Why, Mr. Ludlow!' said Millie reprovingly. 'Most husbands would be honored.'

'Indeed?'

'Why, certainly.' Her blue eyes dwelt on his face, wounded to the quick to think that such a nice gentleman could say such heartless things.

'Okay,' said Tim, thawing. 'I'm honored.'

Sybil's voice was slightly metallic. 'Now that my husband has been won over,' she said, 'I think we may consider the matter settled. The next question is, how do Racy Ruth, or whatever, and I get together?'

'We'd like to have you at the studio no later than three,' said Millie. 'That gives us an hour to line the thing up.'

'It's not extemporaneous?'

'Well, it is and it isn't. Ruth Royce maps the program out in a general way and she gives you a rough idea of how it's supposed to go. That way you avoid unpleasant surprises.'

'Such as?'

'Well, supposing Ruth Royce is asking the girls what they did in England and one of 'em turns out to have been a street walker. It wouldn't sound very well on the air.'

'What would you do? Throw her off the program?'

'Oh, no,' said Millie. 'But we'd make her a hiker. What did you do, Mrs. Ludlow, back in England?'

'Hiked,' said Sybil. 'Are you planning to drive back tonight?'

Millie nodded.

'I was thinking,' went on Sybil, 'that it might be a rather good notion if I drove back with you.'

'Fine,' said Millie. 'Be glad of the company.'

'Where would you stay?' asked Tim. 'You don't just walk into a hotel these days, you know.'

'That's no problem,' said Millie. 'Not for Ruth Royce. She's already got rooms for some of the other brides.'

'In that case,' said Sybil briskly, 'we might as well start before it gets any darker. Why don't you have a drink, Miss Friday, while I throw some things into a bag?'

'Marsden,' said Millie.

'You distinctly said your name was Girl Friday,' said Sybil. 'I'll admit I've never heard of anyone being called Girl, but men are frequently called Boy in England. Always, in Evelyn Waugh.'

'I'm getting confused,' said Millie, 'but I'm darned sure I heard somebody offer me a drink. Have I said 'yes' yet?'

'Perhaps you'd like to tidy up,' said Sybil, 'while Tim fixes the drinks.'

Tim scowled after them as they went into the hall and upstairs. Sure, good old Tim, he'd fix the drinks. And after that he could sit by himself in this House of Usher while Sybil was up to God knew what in New York. She'd certainly jumped at the chance with alacrity, too. With more alacrity than was justified by a silly damned radio program.

He stalked into the kitchen and yanked open the refrigerator door as if he expected to find at the very least a hiding lover.

Above the sound of water running over the ice tray he heard footsteps on the back staircase, and Sybil entered the kitchen. Her eyes were suspicious and angry. 'Tim,' she said, 'that note has disappeared.'

'Note? What note?'

'You know bloody well what note.'

'Where did you leave it?'

'On my dresser. Did you take it?'

'Of course not.'

'Have you any idea who did?'

'How could I?'

'That wasn't the question. Do you?'

Tim concentrated on the ice tray.

'Well?' said Sybil.

'I don't think I'll answer that question,' said Tim. 'I'm not getting answers to many of mine.'

Sybil was silent, tapping her foot. Then she said, 'Very well. But if you have gone behind my back to the police, I will never forgive you.' She went out, and her feet on the stairs sounded weary.

Tim carried glasses, bottles, and ice back to the living room and poked up the fire. Millie Marsden came downstairs and he poured her a drink, showing more solicitude than was altogether necessary for just the right amount of ice and soda.

He poured himself one and they clinked glasses.

'Happy days,' said Millie.

There was an impudence in her face that reminded him of the occasional dimpled co-ed among his students — disruptive, out of place on the course, but nice to have around the classroom.

Sybil appeared a few minutes later, wearing her tweed coat and carrying a light suitcase. 'All set?' she asked.

'All set,' said Millie. 'Be sure and listen in tomorrow, Mr. Ludlow.' *Just you dare and not listen*, the blue eyes added.

'I'll listen,' said Tim. 'Have a good time.'

'Thank you,' said Sybil.

'Give my regards to Broadway,' said Tim.

'Goodbye,' said Sybil.

'Goodbye.'

For a moment they looked at one another, then Sybil crossed the room and kissed him, with cool lips, on the cheek. The front door closed behind the tweed coat and the plaid.

Tim finished his drink with a growing sense of loneliness. The dusk was deep outside the windows, and he walked around the room, turning on lamps and drawing the green curtains. Then he poured himself another drink.

What had happened, anyway, since their joyous reunion in the hotel? Or had it really been joyous on Sybil's part? Was it possible that she had been acting a cunning and wanton role?

So deeply was he sunk in gloomy thought that for several seconds he was unable to grasp the fact that somebody was knocking at the door. His mind brushed the sound aside like a mosquito; then, persistently, it permeated. With a start, half uneasy, half glad of diversion, he went to answer it.

Millie Marsden was standing there, smiling at him trustfully. 'Change of signals,' she said. 'This note explains it.'

She handed him a folded slip of paper and took off her coat while he tried to read without looking at her yellow sweater. The note said:

Tim —
     We stopped to look in on Mr. Square-less. He is running a temperature, and I

think I had better stay with him for a bit, at least until he gets to sleep. Miss Whosit will stay the night. The bed's ready if she doesn't mind Mrs. B.'s sheets, and she better hadn't. You and she can no doubt manage supper between you. Also between you, I'd advise space. I'll walk back later on — S.

'Humph,' said Tim.
'Is something wrong?' asked Millie.
'Nothing important,' said Tim.
The message was written on the same kind of lined tablet paper as the inquest advice of the evening before.

23

Ruddylocks and the Little Bear

'Well, aren't you glad to see me back?' asked Millie.

Tim put the note in his pocket and out of his mind, which was easy in the face of Millie's bright-lipped smile. 'I sure am,' he said, more vehemently than he had intended.

'That's nice,' said Millie. 'How about a little drinkie?'

'Why not?' said Tim.

She walked past him into the living room, brushing him with her shoulder. 'I'll bet you're not really an old crosspatch,' she said, turning by the fireplace and warming her behind.

'Me, a crosspatch?' said Tim, pouring drinks. 'I'm one of the best-natured people you ever met.'

'I thought so,' said Millie.

'Any other impression you may have

255

received,' Tim went on, feeling suave, 'can be blamed on a slight domestic disagreement that arose before your arrival.' He handed her a highball.

'Tsk, tsk,' reproved Millie. 'And you all only married a week or so.'

'Damn it, we've been married two years.'

'Oh,' said Millie. 'That explains it.'

'Explains me being a crosspatch?'

'No, no. It explains why your wife's willing to trust a handsome man like you with a lonesome little girl like me.'

'You, lonesome?' asked Tim with gallant disbelief.

''Course I am,' said Millie. 'No wonder, with all the attractive American men falling for English lassies. Mind you, I don't blame you, but we American gals can't help being jealous, can we?'

Tim leaned an elbow against the mantelpiece beside her. 'I can hardly believe you have much reason to be jealous.'

'Aren't you sweet,' said Millie. Her smile seemed to say that they both knew he didn't mean it but, even so, it did a girl's heart good.

'As a matter of fact,' Tim went on, 'most men would be jealous of me, spending an evening in front of a cozy fire with you.'

'I know one who would,' admitted Millie, chuckling. 'The one who expected to spend the evening with me in a cozy night club. I'm not complaining, though,' she added. 'I take things as they come.'

Tim cleared his throat and studied his drink. 'Actually,' he said, grasping for a change of subject, 'this place isn't as dull as you might think.'

'Who said it was dull?'

'This neighbor of ours,' he plowed on, 'the one who had the accident — what really happened was that he got shot.'

'Really? How?'

'Somebody drew a bead on him through the window. Missed his brains by an inch.'

'How exciting!' exclaimed Millie. 'Do they know who did it?'

'No. But whoever it was, I had my hands on him. Briefly.'

'How thrilling!' cried Millie. 'Tell me.' The blue eyes, accepting the new tack, were wide with interest. Tim told her about it modestly. The eyes became pools of admiration. 'But you were so brave,' said Millie.

'I sort of thought so myself,' said Tim with a grin, basking in her gaze. 'At least, it scares the hell out of me now.'

'You must have been petrified.'

'In a sense. I was knocked cold.'

'Poor thing. You might have been killed.'

Tim gave a shrug — a devil-may-care shrug, he hoped. 'You can still feel the lump,' he said.

'Oh, let me,' said Millie. She stood on tiptoe, putting her left hand on his shoulder to brace herself while her right reached around his bowed head, stroking his hair as it sought the tender knob. 'Oh,' she exclaimed, 'it's enormous. You poor boy.'

Her fingers continued to caress the spot while her other hand tightened almost imperceptibly on his shoulder. Her face was so close to his he could feel her warm breath. The fuzzy yellow sweater touched him.

Tim straightened abruptly. 'Let's have one more drink,' he said, 'and then see what there is to eat.'

'Scaredy cat,' murmured Millie.

'What was that?'

'I said I'd love another little drinkie.'

The little drinkie was duly drunk, and then they investigated the kitchen. Millie suggested they make sandwiches instead of fussing around with a whole big meal. Then they could have another drink with the sandwiches in front of the fire. That would suit him, said Tim.

They sat on the hearthrug with the platter between them. Wind rattled the windows, and rain spattered behind the drawn curtains. The ruddy glow of the fire enfolded them in its light.

'When do you think your wife'll be back?' Millie asked.

'Hard to tell. She said she'd stay with Squareless — the neighbor — until he goes to sleep, and he goes to sleep late.'

'Even when he's been shot?'

'I don't know how that affects his habits. Not much, from what I know of 'em.'

'The reason I ask,' said Millie, 'is because I really ought to stay up for her, out of politeness. But to tell you the truth, I'm just as sleepy as I can be. Must be the ocean air.'

'That'll do it,' said Tim. 'Ocean air and whisky.'

'Here's to 'em,' said Millie, finishing her drink. She stood up, brushing her skirt. 'Guess you'll have to show me where I sleep. I can trust you to, can't I?'

'As you would St. Anthony.'

'I wonder,' murmured Millie. 'Anyway, even if I couldn't trust you, I wouldn't go to that spooky upstairs all by myself.'

'You prefer the known evil?'

She reached down for his arm. 'Come on,' she said, 'you be the lamplighter and go first.'

The upstairs looked pretty spooky to Tim, too, as he went up the sagging staircase. Windows were rattling behind the closed doors and the upper hall was deep in shadow.

'Hurry up and lamplight,' she said. 'I'm getting more scared by the second.'

'What of?' asked Tim with hollow

cheerfulness. He opened the door to the dark bedroom and groped for the switch. It took him an uneasy moment to find it. 'There we are,' he said, standing aside for Millie. 'Damn, the bed isn't turned down.' He said this irritably, though he knew quite well Sybil hadn't expected it to be in use. 'I'll just turn it down for you.'

'Never mind,' said Millie. 'Wait till I'm in it, then you can come tuck me in.' She sat on the edge of the bed and kicked off her shoes and stretched.

'I'll find you pajamas,' said Tim quickly as he went through the connecting door to the other bedroom.

'It doesn't matter,' called Millie. 'I'm used to sleeping raw.'

'You'd better have some,' Tim called back. 'It's a bitter night.' He sounded like a mother hen, he thought, and he wondered if it were a defense mechanism. In the next room, he heard Millie moving about and a rustling that he interpreted as clothes coming off.

'Goodness me,' said Millie, 'I forgot the door was open. Don't peek.'

'I'm looking for pajamas,' said Tim. The only ones he could find were the pale blue pair that Sybil had been wearing. He held them up dubiously and decided they would hardly do for a guest. As he put them back, a sheet of paper fell out of the pocket and fluttered to the floor.

'Don't worry about the old pajamas,' called Millie.

Tim didn't answer. He picked up the bit of paper and read what was written on it in ink:

Imperative I see you alone as soon as possible. Strictly alone. Call me at MU8-1239. Don't worry about a place to stay. I'm taking care of it. Watch your step.

Dimly he heard the soft pad of Millie's bare feet. 'I said don't worry about the pajamas,' she called again.

'What?' asked Tim numbly.

'Never mind. Are you going to tuck me in?'

'Uh huh,' said Tim. Then he blinked and looked up. 'You're damned right I am.'

'Whoa, hold it, St. Anthony,' cried Millie. 'Give me a chance to get under the covers.'

'I'll count ten by fives,' said Tim. His voice was harsh. He heard the squeak of bedsprings and strode into the other room just as Millie snuggled under the blankets, clutching them to her shoulders.

He sat on the bed. 'I'm going to tell you a bedtime story,' he said. 'Once there was a little girl named Reddylocks who found a house in the woods and climbed into bed. Pretty soon, three bears came in.'

'Bears?' said Millie. 'Not wolves?'

'That was Red Riding Hood. Different story. So the first bear, the big one, said, 'Hey, who's sleeping in my bed?' and he pulled back the covers to find out.'

'Ooh,' squealed Millie, tugging at the blankets but not too hard.

'And the second bear, the medium-sized one, said, 'Whoever it is, I'm going to give her a big bear hug.''

'Oh,' cried Millie, 'what a naughty bear he was!'

'And the third bear, the little one — '

'The little bear,' said Sybil's calm and not unamused voice from the doorway, 'cried, 'wee-wee-wee' all the way back to his own bedroom.'

264

24

Status Quo Post-Bedroom

The rain had stopped the next morning, and the sun had come out, but breakfast was something less than jolly. The sunlight was of a cold, pale variety that probed the dining room surgically, resting with particular unkindness on Millie's rather heavy make-up.

She had made a feeble stab at the establishment of a status quo ante-bedroom by remarking that she did declare she'd had so many drinkies the night before, she didn't remember a thing after the sandwiches. Nobody believed her, but it provided her with a line on which to fight it out.

Sybil buttered toast with cool self-possession, as if she were at a table in a crowded restaurant with two strangers from a lower stratum. One passed them the marmalade but one didn't become familiar.

As for Tim, he just sat and suffered.

Any grim satisfaction he might have felt at uncovering damning evidence against his wife had been wrecked by his own ridiculous fall from grace. Certainly he had been in no position to play the outraged husband and face Sybil with the proof of her — of her what? Infidelity? He didn't know. Whatever it was, and aside from his adventures with Reddylocks, he had decided his best move was to lie low in the bushes and see what happened. Meanwhile, he had to sit at the breakfast table in a dignity as shredded as the cereal.

It was a relief all round when departure time came. If any hair-pulling developed en route, thought Tim, at least he'd be well out of it.

'When do you expect to be back?' he asked Sybil.

'I'm not sure. In any case, I'll knock this time.'

Tim felt himself flushing. 'I thought I might meet you at Bankville.'

'I'll take a taxi.'

'What about Squareless? Is he better?'

'I think so. You might look in.'

'All right.'

266

'Anything else?'

'Guess not.'

Sybil bestowed another chilly peck on his cheek.

'Goodbye, Mr. Ludlow,' said Millie. 'Thank you for a simply lovely evening, even if I don't remember it.'

'Goodbye,' said Tim. He waited until he heard the sound of the convertible pulling away from the house, then went into the little library and aimlessly shuffled papers.

★　★　★

The red convertible bowled through the barren streets of Merry Point, across the marshland, and then along the straight sandy road through the pines. Bankville came and went, and the thick, fragrant woods closed in again. For perhaps half an hour, neither woman spoke. Then Sybil, leaning back on the leather seat, said, 'Miss Marsden, we've quite a long trip ahead of us. I'll stop playing wronged wife if you'll stop playing defiant hussy.'

'Defiant hussy!' exclaimed Millie. 'Well, I like that!'

'What would you suggest?'

'Innocent victim,' said Millie blandly. 'After all, I was plied with liquor and chased into bed.'

'I thought you didn't remember that part.'

'I don't. Except like a bad dream.'

'A bad dream?' murmured Sybil. 'Ah well, *de gustibus non est disputandum*.'

'Keep it clean,' said Millie.

'It would be rather amusing,' said Sybil, 'if your Racy Ruth should ask me what I think of American women. Then I could say, well, having found one in bed with my husband last night — '

Millie chuckled but her sidelong glance was uneasy. 'Now, honey,' she said, 'you wouldn't do a thing like that to me, would you?'

'It would ginger up the program.'

'We have incidental music to do that. Kidding aside, Mrs. L., no funny business on the air.'

'You'll admit I'd be justified.'

'I admit no such thing,' said Millie. 'Look, I was tight and I guess your husband was, and nothing happened anyway.

Couldn't we just forget the whole thing?'

'I'm perfectly willing,' said Sybil, 'but I want you to ask me to.'

'Okay. But why?'

'Because I want to ask you something in return.'

'I'm easy to get along with,' said Millie. 'What is it?'

'The thing's complicated,' she said. 'And highly confidential.'

'Oh?' said Millie. 'Is it legal?'

'Mmm, borderline. Tell me, does your job bring you into much contact with newspaper people?'

'Plenty. I've got an ex-husband on the *Times*.'

'Would he know much about the underworld and that sort of thing?'

'No,' said Millie. 'Stamps and pets. That's his field.'

'Oh,' said Sybil. 'Do you know anyone who would know his way about in — well, not underworld circles exactly, but you know what I mean.'

'You mean you're one of those Britishers who wants to meet a real live gangster?'

'Possibly. I want to get in touch with a

man named Jacob Burlick. Perhaps you — '

'Jake Burlick!' exclaimed Millie. 'Honey, that's awful tough company.'

'Do you know him?'

'I don't exactly know him, but I've been to the Breeze Club a few times and met him. He's nobody to fool around with.'

'Well,' said Sybil, 'that's the favor I'm asking. To be put in touch with Jake Burlick.'

'Isn't he in the jug?'

'Out on bail, according to the papers.'

Millie concentrated for a moment on the road. They were out of the pine belt now, and the shuttered hot-dog stands and roadside taverns stood forlorn against the flat meadows. 'Okay,' she said finally. 'I know a guy who could fix it up. When do you want to see him?'

'Soon as possible.'

'Tonight?'

'I thought it might be easier to catch him in the morning. A man who sleeps late, wouldn't you say?'

'If he ever sleeps. You mean this morning?'

'Yes.'

Millie frowned. 'Look, I don't know what you want with this lug, but don't go getting mixed up in anything that'll keep you from the broadcast.'

'Don't worry,' Sybil reassured her. 'How do we go about this?'

Millie looked at her wristwatch. 'Tell you what,' she said, 'there's a cute little bar the other side of the tunnel; we can stop there for a pick-me-up and do some phoning. Now am I forgiven?'

'Thoroughly,' said Sybil.

★   ★   ★

'Cute' wasn't quite the adjective Sybil would have applied to the establishment into which Millie led her. It was located in the lower depths of Greenwich Village, fly-blown and pungent with last night's beer and today's cleaning fluid. Still, it was peaceful and soothing, and Sybil settled gratefully enough to a genteel glass of sherry. And a biscuit. Millie ordered a whisky sour and went into the phone booth.

271

She came back a few minutes later and said, 'B-r-r-r. Where's that drink?'

'No luck?'

'Oh, yes, luck. But the guy I called is a late sleeper, too. Nobody a sheltered girl should phone before noon.' She climbed to a barstool beside Sybil and made a face at her first swallow.

'Here's the dope,' she went on. 'Jake lives in a big apartment across the street from the club. I've written down the address for you. He lives in apartment 6-F, and the idea is you go straight to the sixth floor. Don't speak to the guy at the desk. If he stops you, slip him a fin and say you work for the *News*. If that doesn't hold him, tell him Buck Darcy vouches for you. He's the *News* crime man.'

'Is he the man you phoned?'

'Yeah,' said Millie, 'but let's not go into that. He's got one of these wronged wives, too.' Her blue eyes flickered and Sybil grinned.

'You can use Buck's name on Burlick, too,' continued Millie. 'And Buck says for God's sake to go easy; Jake's jumpy as a rabbit these days. A mean rabbit.'

'Millie,' said Sybil, 'you've been a perfect poppet.'

'Don't mention it. But for the love of Pete, be in that studio at three o'clock, will you?'

'I will,' said Sybil. 'But, Millie — ' She paused and her voice grew serious. 'If by any chance I'm not — and it's a hundred to one — I want you to do something else for me.'

'Boy,' murmured Millie, 'you're sure making that bedroom scene pay off.' Then she sobered. 'Sorry, honey. What is it?'

Sybil reached into her bag and brought out a white envelope. 'If I don't turn up,' she said, 'and if you don't hear from me again by midnight, mail this letter special delivery to my husband. It's stamped and addressed.'

'Okay,' said Millie. She took the letter, then asked, 'How will I hear from you?'

'Have you a phone?'

'Uh huh. It's in the book. Don't call before eleven, though. I got a dinner date.'

'I hope I don't have to call at all.'

'So do I.' Sybil slid off the stool. 'Wish

273

me luck,' she said.

'I wish you in that studio at three o'clock.'

'Hundred to one,' said Sybil. She patted Millie's arm and turned toward the door.

'Wait a minute,' cried Millie. 'Buck said to ask you, are you the gal that testified at some inquest yesterday about meeting a body in your birthday suit?'

Sybil stared. 'How did he know?'

'He says it's in all the papers.'

'Oh, dear God,' said Sybil. 'How pleased Tim's going to be.'

25

A Lady is Missing

Tim's mind was in turmoil, and the mass of notes and diaries and memoranda on his desk reminded him of an occasion when he and another young instructor, after a convivial night, had inadvertently swapped lecture notes and he found himself on the rostrum with pages of indecipherable mathematical symbols in front of him.

It was a relief when a man came to connect the phone. Tim watched him and asked the kind of dumb questions that mechanically inclined people expect professors to ask.

'How about some coffee?' Tim suggested when the man had finished.

'Like to,' the man said, 'but I got another job. Got to fix the phone in that house across the inlet.'

'Squareless's house?'

'Yeah.'

'I didn't think he had a phone.'

'It's unlisted, but he's got one.'

The man packed up his tools and departed. Tim sat at his desk again, but his papers were as meaningless as ever and his distraction was increased by the presence of the shiny instrument in working order. He couldn't get his eyes off it, or his mind off the note in his pocket, the note he had found in Sybil's pajamas. He tried to concentrate on a monograph on the works of Hans Memling. Finally he gave up, pushed the monograph aside, took the note out of his pocket, and stared at the number. Then he lifted the phone and called New York.

The double buzz came and went in the receiver. He was about to hang up when there was a click and a woman's voice said, 'Yah?'

'Who's that speaking?' asked Tim.

'This is the cleaning woman. Nobody home.'

'Look,' said Tim, 'I'm not sure I have the right number. Whose number is this?'

'I told you, this is the cleaning woman. Nobody home.'

'Yes, I know, but who lives there?'

There was a short silence. Then the woman said, 'A fellow what minds his own business.' There was another click.

'Hello, hello,' said Tim, then he put the phone back. He hadn't found out much, but at least it was a fellow. A phrase from his schooldays came back to him: a girl's fellow. Sybil's fellow.

Almost at once, the phone rang. He jumped and looked at it. He had an uneasy feeling that he was about to be accused of something. Of spying on his wife, probably. But the comfortable voice of Mrs. Barrelforth boomed out.

'Hello, that you, Ludlow? Thank God, you've got a phone. Simplifies everything.'

'Where are you?' asked Tim.

'Bankville. I'm on my way over. No, don't bother to fetch me. I'll take a cab. There's hell to pay.'

'What's happened?' asked Tim in alarm.

'Haven't you seen the morning papers?'

'No.'

'I'll read you a couple of headlines. Brace yourself.'

'I'm braced.'

'Here we go, then: Inquest bares war

277

bride's bare dip.'

'My God!' said Tim. 'They don't mean Sybil?'

'Who else? Here's another one: War bride is raw bride as she strolls beach.'

Tim digested this in shocked silence. Then he said, 'Well! Just the background for a professor's wife.'

'I wouldn't know,' said Mrs. Barrelforth, 'but it's a terrible black eye for the Association. I'm coming straight over to give that wife of yours a good talking to.'

'She's not here.'

'Not there? Where the deuce is she?'

'Gone to New York.'

The outraged gusto vanished from the voice at the other end of the wire. Mrs. Barrelforth's next words were businesslike and sharp. 'Did she go alone?'

'No. She went with a girl who works for Ruth Royce Rollick — you know, the radio woman. She's going to appear on the program.'

'Hell's bells,' said Mrs. Barrelforth. 'Why didn't she tell me?'

'She didn't know about it till after you'd left.'

'She could have phoned. Confound it, that's the sort of thing the Association should be consulted about. The way your Lady Sybil carries on, our next batch of brides will think they've nothing to do but run around naked and sing on the radio.'

'She's not going to sing,' said Tim.

'That's beside the point,' snapped Mrs. Barrelforth. 'I'll be there in fifteen minutes.'

* * *

She arrived in twelve minutes, actually, and Tim found himself immediately cheered by the sight of her large red face and billowy tweeds. A drink was promptly requested and promptly produced; then Mrs. Barrelforth wanted to know everything about this ridiculous radio business, from start to finish. Tim described Millie's visit, with suitable omissions.

'Did this Millie girl have credentials of any sort?' asked Mrs. Barrelforth.

'It didn't occur to me to ask her.'

'Look, laddie,' said Mrs. Barrelforth earnestly, 'queer things are going on around here. Credentials, insist on credentials.'

'Right-o,' said Tim. 'Shall we start with yours?'

Mrs. Barrelforth snorted. However, she opened her bag and brought out a small leather case containing a police pass which commended Mrs. Lemuel Barrelforth to the good offices of the authorities.

'Now then,' she went on, 'about this wretched broadcast. We'd better listen to it. What time does it go on?'

'Four.'

'Good. That gives us half an hour to chat. Who, besides you, knows Lady Sybil has gone to the city?'

'Well, Miss Marsden, of course — '

'You referred to her as Millie a minute ago.'

'I did?'

'Yes. Was she pretty?'

'Mmm, so-so.'

'I see. Anybody else?'

'I imagine Squareless knew, because Sybil put off the trip to stay with him last night.'

'All night?'

'No. Just the evening.'

'How about Whittlebait?'

'I don't see how he could have known.'

'Unless Squareless told him,' suggested Mrs. Barrelforth.

'Why should he?'

'I don't know. I was thinking about that mysterious note that either or both of 'em had a chance to plant. Which reminds me, did Lady Sybil mention it being missing?'

'She sure did.' He recounted the acid conversation and Mrs. Barrelforth clucked sympathetically.

'Afraid I put you on the spot,' she said. 'But I thought you'd better know.'

'Speaking of notes,' said Tim, 'I've got a couple of new exhibits.'

Mrs. Barrelforth sat up with interest while he fished in his pocket. 'Sybil sent this from Squareless's house last night,' he explained, handing her the folded slip of paper.

Mrs. Barrelforth looked at it, then brought the other note out of her bag and smoothed out the two of them on her knees. 'Same sort of paper all right,' she said, 'but, on the other hand, it's a garden variety of scratch pad. You'd never hang anybody with this.'

'Cheerful phrase,' said Tim.

'You never can tell,' said Mrs. Barrelforth placidly. 'What's the other exhibit?'

Tim hesitated. 'Maybe I shouldn't have mentioned it,' he said. 'It's on the domestic side.'

'All communications treated confidentially,' said Mrs. Barrelforth. 'Let's have it.'

Tim fingered the bit of paper that had fallen from Sybil's pajamas. 'It probably doesn't mean a thing,' he said.

'Where did it come from?'

'Sybil's pajamas. I dare say some lovelorn laundry worker slipped it into the pocket.'

'I dare say.' Mrs. Barrelforth plucked the note from his reluctant fingers and read it, frowning. Then she exclaimed, 'Why, that's Sam Magruder's number!'

Tim stared. 'By George,' he said slowly, 'that must be the note Magruder gave Sybil at the Breeze Club. She thought she'd lost it. Or did she?' Then he focused on Mrs. Barrelforth. 'How did you know it was his number?'

'My dear boy,' said Mrs. Barrelforth, 'Sam Magruder informed the Association that you needed a place to live. We're in frequent touch. As a seasoned trans-Atlantic traveler, Sam is a great help to the Association.'

'Was a great help, you mean.'

'Why do I mean 'was'?' And now her eyes slowly grew wide. 'My God, are you telling me Sam Magruder is dead?'

Tim nodded.

Mrs. Barrelforth sprang to her feet. 'So that was the body on the pier! Oh, why didn't I guess it? What a bloody fool I've been!'

She began to pace. 'Where's that whisky?' she demanded, finding the bottle as she spoke. She tilted it to her lips and smacked them, but with more grimness than relish. Then she wheeled on Tim. 'Who else knows besides you two?'

'Nobody. Except, of course, whoever killed him.'

'Put it this way. Who knows that you and Lady Sybil know it?'

'No one, as far as I'm aware.'

'Don't be a damned fool. Whoever sent you that billet-doux knows it. Good God, Ludlow, don't you see what this means?'

'I'm not quite sure.'

'It means that your wife is walking around New York with a piece of information that might as well be a time bomb in her pocket. God help her, is all I can say.'

Again she paced, digging her sensible heels into the carpet. Then she looked at her wristwatch and said, 'Turn on the radio. At least we'll know she's safe. Soon as it's over, we'll phone the studio and tell her not to budge till you and I get there.'

Tim switched on the radio and a luscious male voice filled the room. Another chapter had just ended in the life of a young widow named Veronica, who was trying to cope with all the misfortunes one could think of.

'Radio is another problem for the Association,' said Mrs. Barrelforth, sounding normal again. 'Our poor little brides are used to the BBC, which may be dull but never goes poking into one's, uh, privacy.'

Chimes followed, and another voice told them what time it was. The station identified itself. Then still another voice came along and said a few words about corn pads.

The next voice out of the loudspeaker struck Tim as a folksy sort, with a slight twang. It sounded as if the owner didn't give a hoot if she were widely followed or not so long as she could sit down for a homey chat with anybody who cared to listen. It was, of course, Ruth Royce.

'Let's see now, Millie, my dear,' said Ruth. 'What do we have today?'

'Today,' said Millie Marsden's voice, which was considerably crisper than Tim remembered it, 'our program is devoted to a representative group of recently arrived war brides.'

'Ah, yes, the war brides,' murmured Ruth Royce. 'And, my goodness, Millie, aren't they pretty? Stand up, girls, and let me look at you.'

'I can guess how Lady Sybil is reacting to this,' said Mrs. Barrelforth.

'Now, my dears,' went on Ruth Royce's comfortable voice, 'I want to have a little chit-chat with each one of you and hear just what you think about your new life here.'

'I have an awful feeling,' said Mrs. Barrelforth, 'that when your wife steps up to that mike, fifty million radios are going to get blown right out the window.'

A good deal of giggling came from the loudspeaker, then a gummy voice said, 'Well, it's all a bit odd at first, you know, but we've had the flicks, you know. The flicks tell you a fair bit about what the States is like, you know.'

'Flicks?' said Ruth Royce. 'I do hope that isn't a trade name.'

'British for movies, I believe,' said Millie.

'Oh,' said Ruth Royce with relief. 'Next girl, Millie.'

'I can't listen to any more,' said Mrs. Barrelforth abruptly. 'It upsets me. I'm going into the kitchen and drink a drink in decent peace. Call me when your wife comes on.'

The program rambled along with more giggling, a touch of Yorkshire here, a spot of Cockney there, and corn pad ads in between. Tim listened in nervous fascination, the sort of fascination that expectant fathers find in old magazines in hospital waiting rooms.

'Let me see, Millie,' said Ruth Royce,

sounding puzzled, 'I thought we were going to have six of these sweet little brides. But if I can count straight, I only see five.'

'The sixth was unable to be present,' said Millie

'What a shame. Which one was that?'

'Mrs. Ludlow. The former Lady Sybil Hastings, you remember.'

'Ah, yes. Well, let's hope nothing has happened to her.'

'What's that?' asked Mrs. Barrelforth, coming suddenly into the living room. 'Nothing's happened to whom?'

Tim's throat was dry. 'To Sybil. She didn't show up.'

'Hell's bells!' cried Mrs. Barrelforth. 'Where's that phone? Call that radio station! Quick!'

26

Mrs. Barrelforth Means Business

Mrs. Barrelforth stood beside him, cracking her knuckles, while he looked up the station's number and put the call through.

'Ask for that Millie girl,' she said. 'On second thought, it might be better if I spoke to her, woman to woman.' She took the buzzing instrument from Tim. 'What's her last name?' she asked. 'Marsden? Hullo. Miss Marsden, please. That's right . . . Hullo. Miss Marsden? This is Mrs. Lemuel Barrelforth, President of the New Jersey chapter of the British-American War Brides Improvement Association. What? No, I can't say as I did enjoy the program. Never mind that. What I want to know is, what happened to Mrs. Ludlow?'

She listened for a moment, her eyes watching Tim anxiously. He could hear the tinny, perfunctory voice in the phone.

'Now wait a minute, young lady,' snapped Mrs. Barrelforth. 'This is important. It may even be a matter of life and death. If you won't tell me, I'll be obliged to put the whole thing into the hands of the police.'

Again she listened, and a look of grim satisfaction spread over her face. 'She did, eh? What time was that? I see. Righty-o. Thanks very much.'

She hung up and said to Tim, 'Your wife was last seen shortly before noon on her way to call on a man named Jake Burlick. Know him?'

'Jake Burlick?' repeated Tim. 'Isn't that the Breeze Club chap?'

'None other,' said Mrs. Barrelforth. 'Delightful fellow, too. Got plenty of gas in your car? Come on, then.'

Tim grabbed his trenchcoat from the hallstand and followed her through the front door. It was a relief to be going into action, even if he had no idea what that action was going to be. In fact, he was glad that he didn't.

The car was standing where he had left it the day before, and the motor was slow in turning over. He sat there letting it warm up, chafing at the brief delay. The forced passivity of the moment made him want to talk, to ask a question he might not have otherwise asked.

'Mrs. Barrelforth,' he said, not looking at her, 'is my wife mixed up in something she shouldn't be?'

Mrs. Barrelforth's big fingers drummed on her tweedy knees. 'You mean, I suppose, is she a wrong 'un?'

'Something like that.'

'Son,' said Mrs. Barrelforth solemnly, 'I don't know. All I can tell you is this: If she is a wrong 'un, she's as safe as in church. If she's not, and my money says she's not, she'd be safer on a tightrope over Niagara Falls. Let's go. Fast.'

The car roared through the dunes, skidding on the sandy curves, and into the main road. Tim pressed his foot almost to the floor, and the speedometer edged toward seventy and stayed there. The deserted street and big empty houses of Merry Point shot past. They tore across the flat marshland into the cedar swamps' gnarled gloom, then down the straight road through the pines. They slowed briefly for Bankville, which rose in front of them like a sidewalk hitting a drunk, then leaped ahead on the asphalt ribbon through the woods again.

'Ludlow,' said Mrs. Barrelforth presently, 'is that as fast as this jalopy'll go?'

'Just about,' said Tim through clenched teeth.

'I don't know if I ever told you or not,' said Mrs. Barrelforth, 'but as a girl I used to race at Brooklands. What say I take a turn at the wheel?'

'Well . . . ' began Tim doubtfully.

'Slow her to fifty and I'll slide across under you.'

The maneuver was underway before he could protest and completed before he realized it. The speedometer edged up to eighty. It reminded Tim of driving down a German autobahn in a command car with one of Patton's boys at the wheel. Except that this wasn't a command car, the road was no autobahn, and they hadn't conquered the state of New Jersey.

A farm-produce truck nosed out of a side road ahead, saw the juggernaut coming, and stopped cold. Tim closed his eyes, felt the car swerve in a lightning arc, and then opened his eyes to a clear road again. 'Gosh,' he said, 'that was close.'

'Not very,' said Mrs. Barrelforth. 'Only thing you need to worry about is that once in a while, even after twenty years, I forget about driving on the right.'

With this comforting thought, Tim leaned back. He became aware, then, of a growing buzz somewhere behind them. He turned and saw a motorcycle in the fading light. 'Cop,' he said.

'I know, damn it,' said Mrs. Barrelforth. 'Thought I could pull away from him. Well, let's hope he's not the talkative kind.'

She slowed and the motorcycle drew alongside, its rider purple-faced and fuming. Before the latter could pick the adjective he wanted, Mrs. Barrelforth had her leather card-case under his nose and was saying coolly, 'British-American War Brides Improvement Association. Emergency.'

'Huh?' said the cop. He looked at the card, then he looked at Mrs. Barrelforth.

Slowly, and reluctantly, his manner changed. 'Oh,' he said. 'Okay, lady. Sorry.' He even touched his cap.

Mrs. Barrelforth slashed the gears and stepped on the gas again. Tim sank back dazedly on the worn upholstery. It occurred to him that the war brides' husbands had better start organizing if they wanted to survive.

★   ★   ★

They hit the main New York highway, where the heavy traffic of late afternoon slithered along like a great disjointed serpent. The air had grown chill and, in the deepening haze, the sprawling, belching shapes of factories took on a Dante-esque unreality. Mrs. Barrelforth dodged and weaved and blew the horn, picking holes in the converging and diverging lanes like a fullback. Once she turned to Tim and chuckled, 'Can't you just hear 'em back there? 'God-damn woman driver!''

They soared up and over the Skyway as if it had been a thank-you-ma'am, then descended into the turbulent maw of

Jersey City. Soon they were whizzing through the pallid tile-lined tunnel. It disgorged them into a city that even through the shriek and rumble of traffic held a sense of hush as evening fell fast around the tall black outlines of yellow-windowed buildings. Mrs. Barrelforth slid into the streaming tumult of Canal Street.

'Where are we headed?' asked Tim, somewhat limply.

'Burlick's place.'

'Oh,' said Tim.

The damp freshness of the river struck them; then the car was easing swiftly north on the East Side drive, oily smooth under the wheels. It was completely dark by now, and the river glittered with the city's topsy-turvy lights. Tim saw the Empire State's glowing peak go past, then the cluster of shafts and towers that marked Forty-Second Street. A few minutes later they dropped out of the highway swim, back to the prosaic city crisscross. The car slid to a stop in front of a tall white apartment house with a blue marquee and a doorman.

The doorman came forward. 'Sorry,' he

said, 'you can't — '

'Keep an eye on the car, bud,' said Mrs. Barrelforth. 'Come along, Ludlow.'

Tim followed her into a discreetly lit and softly carpeted lobby. A man rose from behind a desk at the far end and said, 'Yes?'

'Yes,' said Mrs. Barrelforth. 'We're going straight up, mac.'

The man looked as if he was going to protest, then thought better of it and sat. The elevator let them off at the sixth floor.

Four doors lined the short corridor, cream-colored and green-carpeted. Mrs. Barrelforth found the one she was looking for and knocked. Nothing happened and she knocked again, harder.

A man's voice said, 'Yeah? Who is it?' It was gruff and suspicious.

'British-American War Brides Improvement Association,' said Mrs. Barrelforth. 'Open up.'

'Nothing doing,' said the voice, which Tim now recognized from faraway mistiness as Jake Burlick's. 'Beat it, or I'll call a cop.'

'That's a laugh,' said Mrs. Barrelforth. 'Open that door, Burlick, or somebody really will call a cop. You'd love it, wouldn't you?'

The door opened a couple of inches, held to that distance by a chain on the lock. Over Mrs. Barrelforth's shoulder, Tim saw in the slit the blue-black sheen of Jake Burlick's hair as it met his eyebrows.

'What's this all about?' asked Burlick.

'We're looking for Mrs. Ludlow,' said Mrs. Barrelforth. 'Is she here?'

'Never heard of her.'

'Rubbish. Open up and we'll have a look.'

'Sorry,' said Burlick. In his mouth, the polite little word was menacing. He gave the door a shove but Mrs. Barrelforth's substantial foot was in it.

'I'm trying to be civil about this,' she said. 'Either we have a nice, informal visit, or I'll get the cops and a warrant. Make up your mind.'

Tim watched Burlick's darkly mistrustful face. Then the chain dropped with a faint rattle and the door opened wide.

'Okay,' said Burlick. 'God knows what good it's gonna do you.'

They found themselves in a rectangular living room, evidently furnished by the management and intended for people of reasonable tastes. The walls were tinted a delicate green and there were several pleasing prints on them. The pastel-shaded furniture was conservatively modern. But the decorator had reckoned without the present occupant's penchant for Kewpie dolls, pin-up girls, and pictures of sports figures clipped from newspapers, or his disinclination to empty ashtrays or remove half-finished drinks or pick up socks.

The occupant himself wore evening dress trousers and a collarless stiff shirt, and over these a bathrobe that looked like a boxer's. An unfastidious boxer's. His blue jowls were wet and smooth, evidently not long shaved. He stood aside with a sullen mockery of a host's bow. Mrs. Barrelforth looked around the room, crossed it, and tried a door that led to the bedroom. She took a turn in the bedroom, which was done in peach, and peered into the rose-tinted bathroom. 'Hmm,' she said. 'Hairpins.'

'So what?' said Burlick from the doorway. 'I ain't no monk.'

'And no Casanova, either,' said Mrs. Barrelforth, walking back to the living room. 'Eh, Ludlow?'

'I wouldn't know,' said Tim. He was looking at Burlick with distaste.

'I've seen you before,' said Burlick, turning on him.

'That's right.'

'You were makin' some kind of trouble. Always makin' trouble, are you?'

'Any trouble I can make for you,' said Tim, 'is a pleasure.'

'Yeah?'

'Yeah,' said Mrs. Barrelforth briskly. 'And we're going to make plenty if you don't start talking.'

'Go ahead,' said Burlick.

Mrs. Barrelforth sighed as if she had hoped that this little unpleasantness could have been avoided. She picked up one of the dreggy glasses from a table and studied it idly for a moment. Then she sent it flying at a round mirror between the draped windows with a splintering crash.

298

Burlick's eyes opened in amazement and rage. He took a step toward Mrs. Barrelforth, his hairy fingers curved in front of him.

'Don't try any rough stuff, sonny,' said Mrs. Barrelforth. 'I'm taking care of the rough stuff. You just answer questions.'

Burlick stood still, looking disgusted and baffled. Tim remembered much the same expression on his face when Sam Magruder had rebuked him in the Breeze Club.

'What's the big idea?' he asked sullenly.

'A small sample,' said Mrs. Barrelforth, 'of the trouble I'm prepared to make if you don't give.'

Burlick looked at Tim as if he expected masculine sympathy. 'Is this dame crazy?' he demanded.

'Maybe,' said Tim, 'but she generally means business. You might as well make up your mind to talk.'

Burlick stared at Tim and then at Mrs. Barrelforth, breathing hard. His face grew sulky and he shrugged. 'What's it to me?' he said. 'Okay. So this Ludlow babe was here.'

'What did she want?'

Burlick hesitated. He looked at the shattered mirror and said, 'She wanted me to put her in touch with Frankie Heinkel.'

'Did you?'

'Hell, I don't even know Heinkel. I don't mess with guys like Heinkel.'

'You don't, eh? Who tipped Heinkel off that Sam Magruder was in the Breeze Club that night?'

'How would I know?'

'Well, that's another story,' said Mrs. Barrelforth. 'What did you do with Mrs. Ludlow?'

'I'm a nice guy when I'm treated right,' said Burlick. 'I sent her to some guys who do know Frankie.'

'Good-hearted Jake,' said Mrs. Barrelforth. 'Mrs. Ludlow didn't happen to mention Sam Magruder, did she?'

Again Burlick hesitated. Then he said, 'Yeah. As a matter of fact, she did.'

'What did she say about him?'

'Said she knew something about him that Frankie Heinkel would like to hear.'

'That's more like it,' said Mrs.

Barrelforth. 'So where did you send her?'

Burlick stared at her for a moment, then suddenly he turned on Tim. He sounded oddly petulant. 'You're the babe's husband, aren't you?'

'I'm the lady's husband,' said Tim.

'All right,' said Burlick. 'She comes along here and she asks me to do her a favor. So I do it. And what happens? You come along and start bustin' up my place. That's what you get doin' a favor. People bustin' up your place.'

'Where is she?' asked Mrs. Barrelforth.

'You want to know? Okay, I'm washin' my hands of the whole damned business. You can talk to the babe herself.'

He crossed the room and picked up an ivory telephone from a low bookcase littered with comic books. He dialed a number and said, 'Jake speaking. Is that limey dame still around? Put her on the wire, will you?' He waited a moment. 'Hello, kid. This is Jake. Look, your husband and some female wrestler are here, bustin' up my place. Will you for Christ's sake call 'em off? Okay.'

He handed the phone to Tim. 'See for

yourself, wise guy,' he said.

Tim took the phone wonderingly. 'Hello,' he said.

'Tim!' It was Sybil's voice, unmistakably. It was sharp, too. 'What in heaven's name are you up to?'

'Looking for you.'

'Well, don't. I'm quite all right. Who's the female wrestler? Mrs. Barrelforth?'

'Who else?'

'Then you and Mrs. Barrelforth go to some nice, quiet pub and drink some whisky. Don't worry about me. I'll explain things tomorrow. I hope.' The last two words were set apart from the hard brightness of the rest.

'Let me speak to her,' said Mrs. Barrelforth.

She reached for the phone, but the line was dead.

27

The Harbor Snuggery

'Satisfied?' Jake Burlick said to Tim.

Tim didn't answer. He stared at Burlick with a dislike so strong that he almost felt sick to his stomach. It filled him with a strange ache to think that this thug should know more about his wife's goings-on than he did. All he wanted to do was hit him.

'I'm not satisfied,' said Mrs. Barrelforth. 'Not by a long shot. How do we know Mrs. Ludlow wasn't talking at pistol point? Where is this place, anyway?'

'What place?'

'The place you just phoned, naturally.'

'Look, lady,' said Burlick, 'when you come in here, you said you wanted to be nice. I've tried to be nice, too. You got what you come for. Supposing you scram.'

'I propose to,' said Mrs. Barrelforth. 'I

propose to scram straight to wherever it was you just phoned.'

'Are you crazy?'

Mrs. Barrelforth smiled and picked up another glass. She gazed at it musingly.

'Listen, lady,' said Burlick, and there was an incongruous note of pleading in his harsh voice, 'those are bad guys. They'd kill me like that if I told you.'

'A very small loss to society,' said Mrs. Barrelforth equably. 'Where's the place?'

'You mean you don't care if I get knocked off?' He sounded shocked and hurt.

'Not especially,' said Mrs. Barrelforth. 'Answer the question, Burlick, or I'll start screaming and charge you with rape.'

Burlick snorted. 'That's one thing nobody'd believe.'

'Oh, I don't know,' said Mrs. Barrelforth, blowing airily on her square fingernails. 'Shall we give it a try?'

'No! For God's sake, no!'

'Then talk.'

Burlick looked out of the window at the tiers of lights against the dark sky. He sighed despairingly and said, 'Okay, sister.

It's a hotel. On West Street. The Harbor Snuggery.'

'Waterfront joint, I take it.'

'Yeah. Fourth floor. Sign on the door says Employees Only, but I don't guess that'll bother you.'

'I don't guess it will,' said Mrs. Barrelforth. 'Especially as you're coming with us.'

Burlick's face looked as if he'd found ground glass in a highball. 'I might as well walk into a firing squad,' he said.

'That's better than waiting for the firing squad to come to you, isn't it?' said Mrs. Barrelforth. 'You'll be safer with us than you will be here. All I want to do is make sure you're not giving us a wrong steer and that you don't warn anybody we're coming. Once we get to this place, you can stay in the car. Get the rest of that monkey suit on and let's go.'

Burlick stared the way people do when a magician borrows and smashes a watch. Like a man in a dream, he got his coat.

★ ★ ★

305

The Harbor Snuggery was a four-story building of weather-beaten frame with dim, unhappy windows and sagging fire escapes. Thick, yellow light seeped out of the ground-floor bar's doors and windows; but it was a sinister, rather than a cheerful, glow.

'Nice place, Burlick,' said Mrs. Barrelforth. 'And God help you if it isn't the right one.' She turned toward the back seat where he had been sitting, but he wasn't there. He was huddled on the floor.

'God help me, anyhow,' he gritted. 'You do some dame a favor and this has to happen.'

'Chin up,' said Mrs. Barrelforth. She and Tim climbed out of the car into the biting wind.

Next to the bar was a separate door over which a sign, illumined by a bulb visible through cracked blue paint, said: Hotel Entrance. Tim followed Mrs. Barrelforth through it and up a flight of dingy stairs. At the top, in a small and evil-smelling space that only the most charitable could have called a lobby, a

306

swarthy man drowsed behind a desk of sorts. He sat up at their footsteps.

'Wrong place, ain't you?' he said softly.

'Don't know yet,' boomed Mrs. Barrelforth. 'We're going up to the fourth floor.'

'Oh, no,' said the man. He sounded sad. 'No, you're not gonna do that. You're in the wrong place.'

'We'll soon see,' said Mrs. Barrelforth. She swept toward the next flight of steps, which rose from a doorway, half-hidden by a rag of a curtain.

Simultaneously the man slid around the desk, moving lithely in spite of his squat bulk. He caught Mrs. Barrelforth's arm. Tim couldn't quite see what happened next, but there was an easy, almost ritualistic movement of Mrs. Barrelforth's large hands and the man leaped into the air with a squeal of pain, described an arc with his legs and went crashing to the floor. He lay there, his eyes open, whimpering.

'Ju jitsu,' said Mrs. Barrelforth to Tim. 'Comes in handy sometimes.'

'Do you teach it to the brides?' asked Tim.

'In extreme cases. Shall we ascend?'

The next floor was illuminated by a naked yellow bulb at the head of the steps and a red one further along, presumably the bathroom. Wallpaper was peeling from the walls and the whole place was acrid with a damp, unwashed smell.

'Must remind Lady Sybil of the old family castle,' said Mrs. Barrelforth. 'One more floor.' She was panting slightly.

Another naked bulb lit the next floor, if you could call it lighting. In the oppressive dimness they could barely make out the sign, Employees Only, on a door at the end of the corridor.

Mrs. Barrelforth knocked. She knocked again. There was no sound. She knocked once more, the beat of her knuckles loud in the silent gloom. 'Looks flimsy enough,' she remarked. 'Let's give it the old heave-ho.'

'Maybe it isn't locked,' suggested Tim.

'Nonsense. Of course it's locked.' She turned the knob, as if to show him his folly, and the door opened. From the darkness came an aroma of good liquor and good cigars, mingled with a fainter

308

odor of good perfume. Mrs. Barrelforth ran her hand along the wall, found a light switch, and turned it on.

It wasn't the luxurious hideaway of a Fu-Manchu, but it was a great deal more comfortable than the rest of the hotel would have suggested was possible. Evidently two of the regular bedrooms had been knocked into one and the walls repapered. There was a sofa that looked new, and a couple of fuzzy easy chairs and a shiny liquor cabinet. In the middle of the room, between two standing lamps, was a bridge table on which a deck of cards lay scattered, while a second deck sat primly beside a score pad in one corner.

'Suffering cats,' said Mrs. Barrelforth. 'Don't tell me your wife's gone to all this trouble just to find a bridge game.'

'Could be,' said Tim. He picked up the score pad. At the top, individual scores marked by initials had been kept. 'Look,' he said. Only one of the scores was plus, and it was plus fourteen hundred points. The initials were S.L.

'Let's hope the stakes were high,' said Mrs. Barrelforth.

28

Speaking of Shots

Mrs. Barrelforth sat in one of the easy chairs near the liquor cabinet, on which stood a half-full bottle of Scotch. 'Might as well try some of this bloke's whisky,' she said. 'Any clean glasses around?'

Tim found two reasonably clean ones and she poured a couple of hookers. 'Here's luck,' she said. 'Although right now we seem to have run out of it.'

Tim's glass paused halfway to his lips. He felt suddenly cold. 'What do you mean by that, Mrs. Barrelforth?' he asked. 'You don't think that Sybil is — is already — '

'No, no,' said Mrs. Barrelforth comfortably. 'I think she's holding her own so far. She's a cool one.'

Tim looked at the bridge table. 'And maybe a wrong 'un?' he asked in a low, strained voice, as if it hurt him.

'Let's not jump to conclusions,' said Mrs. Barrelforth. 'Let us, rather, consider for a moment. Your Lady Sybil wants to see this Heinkel creature in the worst way. Why?'

Tim was silent for a moment. He took a drink of Scotch. Then he said, 'Mrs. Barrelforth, there's something you'd better know. Sybil thinks that Heinkel — '

'Killed her father. Don't look so surprised. I told you, the Association checks up on its brides. But what I don't know is what she has in mind now. Does she want to kill Heinkel with her own hands?'

'Don't,' said Tim. His lean face was white, not looking at her.

'It must have occurred to you,' said Mrs. Barrelforth.

'Of course.'

She glanced at him sympathetically. 'That's pretty good Scotch,' she said. 'Take a big swallow; helps like nobody's business.'

Tim took a big swallow, but it didn't help much.

'Anyway,' went on Mrs. Barrelforth,

'she persuaded good old Jake to get her this far. I think Jake's telling the truth when he says he doesn't know Heinkel. He's just a cheap thug who was used as a combination front man and bouncer for the Breeze Club. If he knew where Heinkel's hiding out, the cops would have hammered it out of him.'

'Mrs. Barrelforth,' said Tim, 'may I ask why the President of the New Jersey chapter of the British-American et cetera is so well up on these matters?'

'You certainly may,' said Mrs. Barrelforth. 'When a little war bride arrives in New York after five thin years, what does she want to do? Make whoopee. And it's when an innocent lassie's making whoopee at places like the Breeze Club that she needs looking after most. So it's up to the Association to be *au courant*.'

'I see.'

'To get back,' Mrs. Barrelforth went on, sipping, 'Lady Sybil got this far. Presumably it took quite a while to fix the meeting with Heinkel, and so they played a little bridge. Why not? What I'm wondering is, did the bridge game break up because they were warned, or simply because it was time to call on Mr. Heinkel? That could be important. Damned important. Because if Heinkel gets the idea that Lady Sybil arranged to be followed — well, not so good.'

Tim put his hands to his forehead. It was wet. Mrs. Barrelforth got up and patted his shoulder.

'Easy, son,' she said gently. 'The Association hasn't given up yet. Not by a long shot.'

Even as she spoke, a sharp crack came from the street below, loud in the dull rush of wind.

Mrs. Barrelforth stiffened like a bird dog. 'Speaking of shots,' she said, 'what did that sound like to you?'

Tim had jumped to his feet. 'My God,' he exclaimed, 'do you suppose — '

'I sure do,' said Mrs. Barrelforth. 'Let's go.'

She paused to empty her glass and Tim was out of the door first. He could hear the clatter of Mrs. Barrelforth's sensible shoes on the stairs behind him as he crossed the dim patch of the first landing and descended fast toward the brighter light of the grimy little lobby.

Rising slowly from the street stairs was the swarthy, squat man. He had a gun in his hand and a look on his face that Tim had seen on G.I.s' faces sometimes when they got used to killing — a cold, nauseating relish.

'Okay, hold it,' the squat man said and leveled the gun at Tim.

Tim didn't exactly hold it. He probably couldn't have if he'd wanted to. His feet paused at about the fourth step, but the rest of him didn't. His eyes saw a round wooden curtain ring and his hands grabbed it, his rangy body swinging into space. His feet sailed into the squat man's face, in which for a second lay dumb surprise; then the face tilted and went backward down the stairs. Only the bottom one was struck, and that with a squashy thud.

Tim dropped to the floor on shaky legs and saw Mrs. Barrelforth calmly picking up the squat man's gun. 'Nice work,' she said. 'I remember Douglas Fairbanks doing something of the sort. We won't see his like again.'

The squat man lay in a heap at the foot of the steps. Mrs. Barrelforth picked her way over him, lifting her skirt a little as if feeling a need to be feminine for a change. 'He'll keep for a while,' she said over her shoulder to Tim. 'But I'm not so sure about poor Jake.'

Poor Jake was still huddled on the floor of the car, but there was a difference. Several differences, in fact, but only one that counted: a round hole where hair met eyebrows.

Mrs. Barrelforth bent over him for a moment, then straightened up. There was a strange expression on her raw-boned face. 'You know,' she said, 'he had it coming to him, all right. But I wish I hadn't said a while back I wouldn't care. It's worse when a bloke's scared.'

29

In the Line of Duty

Tim took a deep breath because he thought it would quiet his nerves, then he realized that his hands were steady and that his nerves were already quiet. His brain, which had been a blur upstairs in the hotel, felt cool and clear. It was a funny thing about death; it did that sometimes. It had been that way in the war, when he'd had to go into a town where there were snipers. Scared green till he got there, then it was all right. Not good, but all right.

'What do we do now?' he asked.

'Cops,' said Mrs. Barrelforth. 'We don't call 'em, though, we go to 'em. Mahomet to the mountain.' She jerked her head toward the hotel entrance. 'And we take that little bundle of trigger-happiness with us.'

They picked the 'little bundle' up

between them and carried him to the car. He was heavy. 'Seems sort of indecent to dump him in back with Jake,' said Mrs. Barrelforth. 'Let's shove him in front.'

They heaved him onto the front seat and closed the door, letting him slump back against it.

'Apparently I get dumped in back,' said Tim.

Mrs. Barrelforth chuckled. 'I've got other plans for you,' she said. 'First place, there's no sense you getting mixed up with the cops. I can handle 'em, but they'll want to know who you are and ask you a lot of questions and maybe even hold you overnight. So I'll wheel our cargo along to Spring Street by myself. Now, don't start a lot of chivalry. It's better that way.'

'I suppose it makes sense,' said Tim. 'I don't like it though.'

'Ah,' said Mrs. Barrelforth, 'but you're going to like what I've cooked up for you. Remember Millie?'

'No use saying I don't,' said Tim. 'But what — '

'Look, I'll be at headquarters for at

317

least an hour. Our pal here should have a lot to tell us when he comes round. Meanwhile, I want you to track down this Millie gal. Find out every damned word Lady Sybil said to her. She must have told Millie something that may help. If she had any sense, she'd have given her a message, just in case. Whatever, find out all you can.'

'I guess so,' said Tim.

Mrs. Barrelforth looked at her watch. 'It's after ten. Phone me at midnight at this number. I'll write it down. Whatever happens, phone me at midnight. Got it?' She handed him a slip of paper and climbed into the front seat of the car beside the limp, squat figure.

'What if that guy comes round too soon?' asked Tim.

Mrs. Barrelforth took from her pocket the gun she had picked up and waved the butt. 'Klonk,' she said succinctly.

The car rumbled off over the rough paving and disappeared into the wide, gaunt darkness of the waterfront street. Tim stared after it with a sinking sense of being left derelict. Then he forced himself to grin. 'There must be better ways to get a Ph.D.'

He decided to head east, the wind ripping round into the side street after him. It was a relief to come, presently, upon a solid and respectable drugstore. Three or four kids who would have looked tough to Tim ordinarily but who looked like Harvard men after the Snuggery were lounging at the soda fountain. Tim walked past them to the phone booth and was pleasantly surprised to find Millie in the book. She lived on Tenth Street. He tried the number but there wasn't any answer.

He went on walking east and realized after several blocks that he was on the outskirts of Greenwich Village, somewhere in the skein of streets that is thrown into chaos by Fourth Street's irresponsible wanderings. He couldn't be too far, then, from Millie's quarters. He went into another drugstore, this one patronized apparently by Oxford dons, and called Millie's number again.

'Hullo,' said Millie's voice. It sounded tired.

'Hullo. This is Tim Ludlow.'

'What!' said Millie. 'Not Tim Ludlow, the well-known bedside raconteur!'

'None other.'

'What brings you to the big city?'

'Oh, one thing and another. I'd like to see you, among other items.'

'I dunno,' said Millie doubtfully. 'I'm just about done in. I've had one hell of a day, with a hangover to start. I suppose you know your little woman didn't turn up for the show.'

'Yes. I was listening.'

'She put me in an awful hole,' said Millie. 'The timing was messed up and so was the script, and of course Ruth Royce blamed me. What happened to Lady Sybil?'

'She got involved in a bridge game, apparently.'

'What! How do you know?'

'I talked to her on the phone a while ago.'

'Well, I'm damned.' Millie's voice was irritated. 'I'm double-damned. You know, that burns me up a little.'

'Me, too. In a way.'

He sensed the change in her tone when she next spoke. 'We might as well burn up together,' she said. 'I don't feel like going anyplace, but we could have a drinkie at my shack.'

'Fine.'

'Can you find your way to Tenth Street?'

'I'm somewhere around there now,' said Tim.

'Counting your chickens, were you? Hurry up, then.'

After he'd hung up, it occurred to Tim that he might have given Millie a misleading impression of his state of mind.

Her apartment was in a three-story brick building with two bare trees in front of it. He rang the bell marked Marsden and waited for the buzzer. It buzzed and he pushed open the white-painted door with its useless brass knocker and saw Millie standing in the soft hall light at the head of red-carpeted stairs. She was wearing a flowered housecoat with flaring skirt and sleeves, but otherwise molded to her charms. As he came up the steps, he noticed that it was the kind of housecoat that zips down the front.

'Take your eyes off that zipper,' said Millie, 'and come in.'

It was a one-room apartment with a studio couch on which colorful pillows were piled. The curtains were colorful, too, and there were bright modern prints on the walls and bright covers of books in white bookcases between the windows. On a low table in front of the couch stood a cocktail shaker and two glasses.

'I've made us a mess of whisky sours,' said Millie. 'Hope you like 'em.'

She hung his trenchcoat on the back of the door and they sat together on the couch. Millie poured smooth golden liquid from the shaker. 'Here's to the three bears,' she said, holding her glass to his.

'Here's to 'em,' said Tim. He couldn't think of anything else to say.

'Here's to the little one, in particular,' said Millie. 'I never did find out what he was going to do to Reddylocks.'

'It's a continued story,' said Tim. Damn, that wasn't what he'd meant to say.

'Oh?' said Millie. She leaned back

luxuriously on the cushions and looked at him over the rim of her glass.

Tim cleared his throat. 'Millie,' he said, 'before — before we — '

'Before we what?' asked Millie. Her voice scolded him but her eyes didn't.

'Before we drink these drinks,' said Tim, 'I've got to ask you something.'

Millie sighed faintly. 'Go ahead,' she said. 'My life's an open book. Banned in Boston, but open.'

'It's not about your life. It's about Sybil's.'

Millie frowned. 'If you've come here for a sisterly talk about how your wife misunderstands you, I'm not interested.'

'I haven't.'

'You're sure?' As she spoke, she rolled slightly toward him and lifted her face until it was a few inches from his.

'Yes.'

'I'm from Missouri,' she said. Her voice was husky, her bright lips close.

Well, thought Tim, *line of duty*. He moved his head forward, stiffly as in the *mouvement de danse* known as pecking, and her mouth crushed against his. Her

323

arms went round his shoulders and she pulled him back among the pillows.

Then suddenly she released him and pushed him away, not angrily but with a kind of rueful playfulness. 'Little bear,' she said, 'you've got something on your mind. When a guy kisses me and thinks about something else, he's got a lot on his mind.'

'I can believe it,' said Tim. 'And I guess I have.'

'All right,' said Millie. 'Spill it.'

'Did Sybil tell you where she was going?'

'Yes. And she said it was strictly confidential.'

'I see. But couldn't you —— '

'No. I don't blab other women's secrets. Not even when they're the wives of guys I could go for.'

'Look, Millie,' said Tim, 'I know Sybil went to see the late Jake Burlick. But you —— '

'Whoa!' cried Millie. 'The *late* Jake Burlick?'

'Yes. He was shot dead about an hour ago.'

'Oh my God,' said Millie. She sank

limply back on the couch and stared at him with wide, shocked eyes. 'It wasn't — it wasn't — '

'It wasn't Sybil.'

'Thank God for that,' said Millie. 'Or I might have been an accessory before the fact.' She pushed herself to her feet and walked nervously around the room. 'This puts a different complexion on things,' she said. 'What time is it?'

Tim looked at his watch. 'Three minutes to midnight.'

'At midnight,' said Millie, 'if I haven't had word from your Lady Sybil, I'm supposed to mail you a special delivery letter. I wasn't going to tell you.'

'Have you got it?'

'Wait till midnight.'

They sat there silently. Tim could hear the tiny tick of his watch.

'My God,' said Millie suddenly, 'this is the longest three minutes I ever spent. You might kiss me again, just to pass the time.'

The minutes picked up speed.

Tim stood up, blinking a little dazedly. 'It's midnight,' he said, but for a moment he couldn't remember what difference it made. 'Midnight,' he repeated, and then he remembered. 'I've got to make a phone call.'

Millie stared. 'Not — not to your wife?'

'No. Another woman.'

'Well, I'm damned,' said Millie. 'Maybe I've underestimated you. The phone's in the kitchenette. Here's the letter.'

She handed him the envelope, addressed to him in Sybil's handwriting, in pencil. He looked at it and turned it over. He realized that he was afraid to open it. 'Where'd you say the phone was?' he asked.

'Kitchenette. That door.'

He closed the door behind him and dialed the number Mrs. Barrelforth had given him. Her comforting boom answered. 'Minute late,' she said. 'Line of duty, I suppose. Any news?'

'Yes,' said Tim. 'Sybil left a letter with Millie. She was supposed to mail it at midnight to me if she didn't hear from Sybil.'

'Have you got it?'

'Yes.'

'What does it say?'

'Haven't opened it yet.'

'Then open it, for God's sake.'

He tore the envelope open and unfolded the letter. His fingers weren't steady any more. The letter said:

Tim, darling:

At last you can do what you've wanted to do all along. As soon as you get this letter, notify the New York police that the body we found on the pier was Sam Magruder's. Tell them everything else you can that will help them run the Heinkel gang to earth. Because that's where I'll be.

If I'm lucky, I'll be able to explain everything to you. If I'm not, just remember this: I love you, I love you, I love you.

'Read it to me,' said Mrs. Barrelforth.

Tim couldn't find his voice for a moment. The words swam in front of his eyes. On his dry lips, the taste of Millie's lingered like wormwood.

'What's the matter?' demanded Mrs. Barrelforth.

'Nothing,' said Tim. He read the letter aloud, his voice jerky and mechanical like that of a boy orator with stage fright. When he came to the last sentence, he stopped, choking. 'She closes with an expression of affection,' he said.

'I see,' said Mrs. Barrelforth. 'Where's that hussy's flat?'

'Tenth Street.'

'D'you know the big drugstore at the corner of Eighth Street and Sixth Avenue? Meet me there fast as you can. I've got news, too.'

30

In a Crumpled Heap

'Everything all right?' asked Millie.

'No,' said Tim. 'I've got to go.'

'Better have a drinkie.'

'No, thanks.'

She smiled at him, a twisted little smile. 'Gonna kiss me before you go?'

He hesitated, then stepped forward and kissed her quickly on the cheek. She caught him by the lapels and clung to him, her face nuzzling his. The sultry fragrance of her body made him dizzy. He took her wrists and looked down at her. Under the make-up, her face was old.

'Goodbye, Millie,' he said.

'Ah, hell,' said Millie to the ceiling. 'Why do I always get mixed up with husbands? Goodbye, St. Anthony.'

The sharp wind that shook the branches of the two bare trees outside felt good. Tim pulled his trenchcoat around him and walked fast down the street.

Sixth Avenue was garish with neon. At the corner of Eighth Street people were buying morning papers at a stand, their chilly faces and turned-up coats caught briefly in the glow from the big drugstore. Inside, there was a crowd at the long fountain from which rose the pungency of sticky syrups and mayonnaise and coffee. A fat woman in slacks with a dog on a leash browsed through the cut-rate books. To Tim, as he stepped inside, the life and warmth of the place seemed abruptly unreal, as if he had wandered from an alley through a stage door and onto the set. There was no sign of Mrs. Barrelforth.

Tim found a seat at the fountain and ordered coffee. Somebody had left a tabloid on the sticky marble. He picked it up idly while he waited, and a headline on a small boxed item caught his eye: 'There Goes That War Bride Again.'

Tim gulped and read on:

'That titled English war bride who caused a courtroom commotion with her story of a beach stroll in the altogether was still making news yesterday. At the last minute, Mrs. Timothy Ludlow, the former Lady Sybil Hastings, failed to show up for a scheduled appearance on the Ruth Royce Rollick radio program. It was learned that she drove to New York earlier in the day but apparently got lost in the big city. One school of thought suggested she'd gone for a dip in Central Park. Anyway, efforts to locate her failed.'

A hand touched Tim's shoulder and Mrs. Barrelforth's voice said, 'Ah, black coffee. That's the ticket.'

Tim pointed to the news item. 'By Jove,' said Mrs. Barrelforth, 'that's a break for us. And, son, we need every break we can get.'

He looked up anxiously. 'Has anything happened?'

'That hotel mug finally saw the advantages of unburdening himself. I'll tell you in the car. Finish your coffee.'

It burned his throat. 'Where are we going?' he asked.

'Merry Point. Come on.'

She led the way to a long black sedan that was double-parked beyond the

331

newsstand. 'Hey,' said Tim, 'where's my car?'

'In good hands,' said Mrs. Barrelforth, climbing in. 'I've borrowed this one for the time being.'

'Why?' asked Tim, as her foot on the accelerator stroked the motor's purring back. The big car slid silently into the intersection traffic.

'I figured yours might be recognized,' said Mrs. Barrelforth. 'They've had a good look at it and it's not hard to arrange an accident when you know how. As Lady Sybil's father found out.'

The car rushed smoothly south into comparative darkness and stillness.

'By 'they' do you mean the Heinkel bunch?' asked Tim.

Mrs. Barrelforth nodded.

'But why would they lay for me?' Tim asked her. 'I'm a strictly innocent bystander.'

'Not since you got that letter,' said Mrs. Barrelforth grimly. 'You're hot cargo, son.'

The bluish dimness of the plaza in front of the tunnel loomed ahead.

'How could they possibly know I've got the letter?' asked Tim.

'You cloistered scholars can be awfully slow,' said Mrs. Barrelforth impatiently. 'The letter was Lady Sybil's safety play. She knew jolly well she'd never leave Heinkel's hideout alive if he thought the story of Sam Magruder's death would die with her. So naturally she told Heinkel that if anything happened to her, you'd get the letter.'

'Oh,' said Tim. The car was roaring through the tunnel now, its tires loud on the flooring.

'Of course,' went on Mrs. Barrelforth, 'this bit of publicity in the papers helps, too. There might be a little too much interest in Lady Sybil now for her to disappear without a fuss.'

'Damn it,' said Tim, 'I'd make a fuss if she disappeared.'

'I am suggesting,' said Mrs. Barrelforth, 'that otherwise you might both disappear. There's nothing easier to get rid of than a couple of honeymooners. They're expected to disappear now and again.'

Tim thought this over in growing

uneasiness. It made sense, all right; fantastic sense, but sense. The car rolled through the wide, barren streets of the Jersey side between dark and silent buildings.

'However,' said Mrs. Barrelforth, with a return of her customary boom, 'they reckoned without the British-American War Brides Improvement Association. Especially the New Jersey chapter.'

Tim grinned to himself, then suddenly the grin froze. A hideous thought struck him like ice. What if Mrs. Barrelforth was on the other side? If, even now, he was being carried to some terrible and final rendezvous?

Now, wait, said the sensible shreds of his mind. *The woman obviously enjoys the best of relations with the police.*

Ah, yes, came back the new and ugly thought, *but don't forget the Breeze Club enjoyed police immunity. Political connections, bribery, corruption — that was the picture.*

He glanced warily at the large, raw-boned face beside him. In profile, with the jaws set as she drove, it looked hard. But it looked honest.

The big car sailed up the Skyway, high above the winking lights and ruddy glow of strange nocturnal industries.

'Why are we going to Merry Point?' asked Tim.

'Because that's the target area,' said Mrs. Barrelforth. 'Our friend spilled that much. Trouble is, he doesn't know where the actual hideout is. All he knows is that when he gets instructions from Heinkel, they come by phone from a Bankville number. That doesn't necessarily mean Merry Point, of course, but it's around there. Who else has a phone in your neighborhood, anyhow? Squareless doesn't, I remember.'

'Yes, he does,' said Tim.

Mrs. Barrelforth looked at him and whistled softly. 'I'll be blowed,' she said.

Another chill thought struck Tim, more frightening than the other because it was more grotesque. 'Mrs. Barrelforth,' he said, and his voice sounded small to him, 'has it occurred to you that — that Squareless's housekeeper might be a man?'

'Not possible,' said Mrs. Barrelforth.

'Of course, there were those stories in England about spies dressed as nuns, but — no, it's not possible. Any other phones around there? How about that general store you mentioned?'

'No phone there,' said Tim. Then something clicked in his mind. 'Although, by God,' he added, 'something that sounded like a phone rang in the back room when Sybil and I were there. The storekeeper said it was an alarm clock.'

'What time was it?'

'Around eleven.'

'Damned odd,' said Mrs. Barrelforth. 'Well, these are matters to be borne in mind. Meanwhile, Ludlow, there should be one bright spot on your horizon.'

'What?'

'I'd say, offhand, that the letter proves one hundred percent that your Sybil is no wrong 'un.'

'Yes,' said Tim, half to himself. 'Yes. If only she's a live 'un.'

Behind them the Skyway rose in a majestic sweep of pinpoint lights against the gray-black sky. Ragged threads of the cold night air rushing past curled into the car, damp and chill and full of foreboding. Tim huddled inside his trenchcoat.

★　★　★

An hour and a half later, the road broke out of the cedar swamps as if glad to escape their oppressiveness. Across the salty gray marshland ahead of them lay the sharp, black shapes of Merry Point's empty houses. In the distance, on the rising tip of land above the inlet, they could see pale light in John Squareless's house. The house on the opposite bluff was dark.

Mrs. Barrelforth slowed the car and turned off the lights. 'I've got a gun,' she said. 'Just in case. Can you handle one?'

'Not happily, but I can.'

She thrust the cold metal into his hands. 'Don't use it unless I tell you. No telling what you might hit.'

The car glided silently through the ghostly main street and crossed the white bridge slowly with scarcely a rumble. Mrs. Barrelforth drove past the driveway and came to a stop a hundred yards further on in the shadow of overhanging dunes.

'We'll do better on foot,' she said. 'No telling who might be expecting us.'

They slipped and skated in the loose sand as they pushed through the dunes. The wind whipped the long beach grass around their legs and sent stinging gusts of sand into their faces. Cat-briars caught at their clothes. Close but invisible, the surf licked at the sandbar on the beach below the house, which now rose in front of them, windswept and bleak.

Mrs. Barrelforth caught Tim's arm. 'Something moved beside the porch,' she whispered. 'See it?'

Tim strained his eyes through the murk. The gravel of the driveway was pale against the dark shapelessness of the bushes. He couldn't see anything that moved. 'By the steps,' whispered Mrs. Barrelforth. 'See?'

'No.'

'You will in a second. Point your gun that way.' She brought a flashlight out of her pocket and sent a dazzling beam against the porch steps. Besides the steps, crouched in the bushes, was a human figure.

'All right,' called Mrs. Barrelforth in a brisk, cool voice, 'get 'em up and walk this way. You're covered.'

Slowly the figure straightened up, tall and muffled.

'My God,' said Tim, 'it's Squareless's housekeeper.'

The woman turned her gaunt face, pale and suddenly grateful, toward him. 'Is that Mr. Ludlow?' she called. 'Thank God!' She came toward them, pulling her cloak around her in the wind.

'What are you doing here?' asked Mrs. Barrelforth.

'Mr. Squareless saw a car drive up a little while ago.' She was breathing hard. 'Then it drove away again. He was afraid something was wrong. He sent me to see.'

'And *was* anything wrong?' asked Mrs. Barrelforth. Her fingers still held Tim's arm and they were tight.

'Yes,' said the housekeeper. 'Look.' She turned toward the porch and pointed. Mrs. Barrelforth sent a beam of light shimmering in the direction of the woman's finger.

In front of the door, in a crumpled heap, lay Sybil.

31

Attached Find One Wife

'She's alive,' said Mrs. Barrelforth, on her knees beside the inert form. Tim, kneeling too, couldn't speak.

Mrs. Barrelforth shone the flashlight on Sybil's face and forced an eyelid open. Then she sniffed at her lips. 'Chloral hydrate,' she said. 'Let's get her inside.'

Tim's hands were shaking so much, he could scarcely get the key into the lock. The rush of relief after those seconds of thinking his wife had come home as clay was almost too much for him. He leaned dizzily against the wall while his hand felt weakly for the light switch. Light and the warm familiarity of hall and living room steadied him a little. He turned back toward the porch, but Mrs. Barrelforth was already coming in with Sybil in her arms.

She laid her on the wicker settee

opposite the fireplace and loosened her clothes. 'Get a fire going,' she said to Tim. 'The child's cold as ice. And coffee.' This was to the housekeeper, who had followed them in. 'Lots of coffee.'

Julia didn't seem to hear her. She was staring down at Sybil's clammy white face and disheveled dark hair and twisting her bony hands. Then she realized she had been addressed. 'What?' she said. 'What did you say?'

'Coffee,' said Mrs. Barrelforth. 'Gallons of it.'

Julia nodded and went out, pausing at the doorway to look back once more at Sybil. Mrs. Barrelforth glanced after her thoughtfully, then she turned her attention to Sybil again. 'Hullo,' she exclaimed, 'what's this?'

A white envelope protruded from the pocket of Sybil's rumpled coat. Mrs. Barrelforth looked at it and handed it to Tim. 'Addressed to you,' she said.

Tim got up from the fireplace, where a cheerful crackle was rising, and ripped open the envelope. Inside was a note written, again, on lined tablet paper.

'If it's not too personal,' said Mrs. Barrelforth, 'you might read it aloud.'

Tim read: 'Mr. Ludlow — Attached, find one wife in better condition than you or she has any right to expect. There's nothing wrong with her a little sleep won't cure. But the next time you or she pokes a nose into something that is none of your damned business, it will be a different story. The smart thing for you two to do is to get the hell out of this locality and forget everything you ever knew or guessed about bodies on piers or anything else. This is friendly advice. If it becomes necessary to bring the matter up again, it will be on a slightly different basis. Better get started.'

'Hmm,' said Mrs. Barrelforth. 'That last bit sounds like an advertisement, doesn't it? Clip the coupon now.'

'You'll forgive me,' said Tim, 'if I don't laugh.'

'I do my best laughing in times of stress,' said Mrs. Barrelforth. 'On the other hand, nobody has told me to move in the middle of a housing shortage. That could be serious.'

Julia came back into the living room. 'The coffee will be ready in a moment,' she said. 'If you don't mind, I feel I should get back to Mr. Squareless.'

'That's right, he's an invalid, too,' said Mrs. Barrelforth. 'I'd almost forgotten that.'

She walked across the room toward the housekeeper, then stumbled over her own feet and fell against the other woman. Julia gave a little cry.

'So sorry,' said Mrs. Barrelforth, regaining her balance. 'I must have tripped on the rug. Do forgive me.'

'Certainly,' said Julia. Her cold expression made it clear that she thought Mrs. Barrelforth had been drinking. 'If there's nothing more, I'll be going.' She bowed slightly with austere dignity and went out.

'It's rather convenient sometimes,' said Mrs. Barrelforth, 'to have a reputation for tippling. Which reminds me, it's been a long time. Anyway, you don't have to worry about the housekeeper's gender anymore. It's the genuine article.'

343

32

The Rest of the Story

Tim woke up to a day that was bright and clear and cold. The ocean lay, an untroubled blue, outside the bedroom windows and, for a moment, the night's events seemed but the evanescing blur of an evil dream. Sybil's dark head was beside him on the pillow and, as he looked at her with sleepy relief, her eyes opened, puzzled at first, then gradually content. They were still a bit bleary, though, and her face was pasty.

'Am I really here?' she asked.

'Yes, dear,' said Tim.

'Did somebody knock? Or did I dream it?'

A light tap sounded on the door.

'Somebody knocked, I guess,' said Tim. He raised his voice. 'Who is it?'

'Me,' came the familiar Barrelforth boom. 'I've brought you slugabeds some coffee.'

The door opened and the President of the New Jersey chapter appeared, wrapped once again in Tim's old bathrobe. She was carrying a tray which she set down on the bedside table. 'Shall I pour?' she asked. 'How do you feel?'

'Groggy but good,' said Sybil. 'How did I get here?'

'Special delivery,' said Mrs. Barrelforth. 'Drink a little coffee and maybe you can tell us where you last remember being.'

Sybil drank a little coffee. 'I'm not sure where I was,' she said.

'That may be,' said Mrs. Barrelforth, 'but you were with Frankie Heinkel, were you not?'

'So I was given to understand.'

'I don't mean to press you, my dear,' said Mrs. Barrelforth, 'but there are certain matters that have got to be cleared up right away. What did you do after you left the Harbor Snuggery?'

Sybil looked from her to Tim. 'So you found the Snuggery, did you?' she murmured. 'Charming spot, what?'

'Still,' said Mrs. Barrelforth, 'bridge, like a honeymoon, is fun anywhere, isn't

345

it? If you like bridge.'

Sybil chuckled. 'Won a hundred and forty dollars,' she said complacently.

'While you were waiting for a meeting with Heinkel to be arranged?'

'Yes.'

'Using the murder of Sam Magruder as a letter of introduction, you might say?'

'Yes.'

'So what happened?'

Sybil sipped her coffee. 'First,' she said, a little tremulously, 'there was the phone call from Jake Burlick. When I talked to you.' She turned regretful eyes on Tim. 'You'll understand, in a minute, that I couldn't do anything else.'

'I'm not worried,' said Tim.

Sybil smiled gratefully. 'Then,' she said, 'the word came through that Heinkel was waiting to see me. We got into a car and then, quite politely I must say, I was blindfolded. And we drove for a long time. I've no idea where, but I thought I smelled pines.'

'Then what?'

Sybil's tongue ran over her lips as if she were trying to identify a bad taste. 'Then,'

346

she said slowly, 'we stopped and went into a house. At least, I suppose it was a house. It was warm and it smelled like a place people lived in. Not very tidy people.'

'You were still blindfolded?'

'Yes, the whole time. Then somebody said, 'Frankie, this is the lady who wants to talk about Sam Magruder.''

'Reminds me of Dorothy's first interview with the Wizard of Oz,' said Mrs. Barrelforth. 'What happened next?'

'We talked.'

'What about?'

Sybil hesitated. 'Personal matters,' she said.

'Sybil,' said Tim gently, 'perhaps I should tell you that Mrs. Barrelforth knows about your father.'

'Oh,' said Sybil. Her eyes grew faintly reproachful. 'Did you — '

'No,' said Tim. 'She already knew. That's what you talked about, wasn't it?'

'Yes,' said Sybil softly. 'We talked about my father.'

Mrs. Barrelforth waited a moment, then demanded impatiently, 'Well?'

'That's all,' said Sybil.

347

'Rubbish,' said Mrs. Barrelforth. 'You offered to trade what you knew about Sam Magruder, plus a pledge of silence, for something Frankie Heinkel knows about your father. Right?'

'Roughly.'

'How did it work out?'

'Not very well. First, Heinkel wanted to know who else knew about Magruder, and I told him nobody; but that the police would know if anything went wrong.'

'Jolly good thing, too,' said Mrs. Barrelforth. 'By the way, did Heinkel's voice sound familiar?'

'It's strange,' said Sybil, frowning. 'For a while I thought it did, then I decided it didn't. Did you ever feel that way at a masquerade?'

'Can't say as I have,' replied Mrs. Barrelforth. 'Go on.'

'There isn't much more. Mr. Heinkel proceeded to give me a pompous little lecture on how foolish I was to involve myself in his affairs. He said he didn't trade information; he suppressed it. Then somebody shoved something to drink at me and that's all I remember.'

'You were pretty lucky, at that,' said Mrs. Barrelforth.

'Was I?' said Sybil bitterly. 'I didn't get what I'd risked everything for.'

'What was that, dear?' asked Tim.

Sybil was silent for a while. Then she spoke with an effort. 'When Daddy went away the last time — went away knowing it might be the last time — he told me that if anything went wrong, there would be a message. A very important message. Something that would change everything. He didn't say how he would get it to me. Perhaps he thought they — they'd give him more of a chance.' She turned her face away and wept quietly into the pillow.

Mrs. Barrelforth touched her shoulder. 'Lady Sybil,' she said, 'the time has come for you to tell your husband the rest of the story about your father.'

Sybil continued to press her face to the pillow. Then she lifted it, white and stained. 'Yes,' she said, and her voice was calm, 'I suppose it has.' She sat up in the bed and looked at Tim with a kind of sad but yet defiant pride. 'Remember,' she said, 'I never told you my father was the

349

earl of anything. He wasn't. He was a professional shipboard gambler.' She paused, watching Tim's troubled face. 'He acquired himself a title,' she went on, 'because it made it easier for him to slide into the most exclusive, and richest, card-playing circles. Especially, if you'll forgive me, among your compatriots.'

Tim gazed into his coffee cup, then automatically lifted it to his lips, though it was empty.

'Poor Tim,' said Sybil. The hard brightness, like a defense against emotion, crept into her voice. 'It came as a great shock to me, too, if that helps. I didn't know till I was eighteen. First Santa Claus, then the stork, and then — this.'

Tim still stared at his cup. Mrs. Barrelforth took it from him and filled it. 'Go on,' she said.

'You see,' said Sybil, 'I never saw much of Daddy until I grew up. I lived with an aunt, his sister, and all I knew was that my father's affairs required him to travel a great deal. It was a frightfully normal girlhood, really. There wasn't any nonsense about a title, and I turned out to be rather good at field hockey. And quite fetching in a field hockey costume, which is difficult. The only unusual thing about my adolescence was Daddy's insistence, whenever he was home, that I learn to play bridge. I liked it, too. May I have some more coffee, please?'

Mrs. Barrelforth filled her cup.

'When I was eighteen,' Sybil continued, 'Daddy took me on one of his trips. You can imagine the thrill. And on top of the excitement of a luxury liner, I found out that I was supposed to be Lady Sybil, instead of plain Sybil, or even Syblet, as I'm afraid I was called. Daddy explained that he'd never told me because he hadn't wanted me to grow up apart from other girls.

'It was a lovely trip in the Mediterranean, and everybody was so gay. That was when I met Sam Magruder. And, of course, there was a great deal of bridge. I didn't even know what the stakes were. Daddy would always carry me. It made him seem fearfully honest — the distinguished gray-haired earl, accompanied by his charming and innocent daughter.'

351

'Did you play innocent bridge?' asked Mrs. Barrelforth.

'Yes,' said Sybil. She spoke with fierce emphasis. 'My father wasn't the sort who cheated. He didn't have to. He used to say — ' Her eyes grew fond. ' — that it wasn't the Great God Luck, it was the Great God Percentage.'

'Nevertheless,' said Mrs. Barrelforth, 'he was using you as a confederate. By his lights, perhaps, he was honest. But he had no right to use you for his — I can't think of any other word — skulduggery.'

'Perhaps,' said Sybil, 'but I loved him.' She was silent for a moment, struggling to regain her composure. 'I must admit,' she continued, 'that my aunt was of our opinion. After we came back from our cruise, she cornered Daddy. I was upstairs, but I could hear a hot and heavy row going on. The next day, my aunt told me the truth. It wasn't a very happy day in my life.' She glanced sideways at Tim, as if hoping for a sign of sympathy in disillusionment. He didn't look at her.

'I faced Daddy with it,' she said. 'I had to. But it was pretty dreadful. He cried.

And, of course, I did. I don't like to think about it. In the end, he swore he'd give the whole thing up, but he had to make one more trip. He just had to. Then he told me he was in a spot of trouble. That's all. And that there'd be a message if he didn't come back.'

She stopped and shrugged. 'Well, he didn't come back. Whoever he was afraid of got him. And at the same time, the man all Europe was afraid of got Poland. I went into the ATS, and I went in with everything I had. It's a terrible thing to say, but the war, in a way, was a relief to me.'

'Your aunt,' said Mrs. Barrelforth. 'Did she know what the message was?'

'I don't know. I didn't see her for some time after I went into the ATS. Then one day she phoned me and said she was going to the States. To look into Daddy's death, presumably. Perhaps she was looking for the message, too.'

'Did she find it?'

'She sailed on the *Athenia*,' said Sybil quietly. 'She wasn't — among the survivors.'

There was another silence in the sunlit clarity of the room.

'That's the story,' said Sybil. 'I made up my mind to get to the States as soon as the war was over. Marrying an American made it easier.'

'Was that why you married him?' asked Mrs. Barrelforth.

'By a curious coincidence,' said Sybil — and under the hard brightness, her voice trembled, 'I was in love with him. I still am. But I haven't much right to expect that he's still in love with me.'

For the first time in quite a while, Tim spoke. 'Mrs. Barrelforth,' he said, 'there seems to be some doubt on my wife's part as to whether I'm in love with her or not. Would you mind — '

'I don't have to be told when I'm *de trop*,' snapped Mrs. Barrelforth. 'I'm just trying to get the coffee things out of your way.'

33

A Way to Die

The wind came up and drove gray clouds across the sky, dousing the sunlight and turning the ocean to slate, but it could have blown the roof right off the bedroom without the occupants taking much notice. Mrs. Barrelforth had to knock several times before she got a reply.

'I don't know how long it takes young people nowadays to kiss and make up,' she boomed through the door, 'but you're well past the limits fixed by the Association. Besides, you have guests.'

There was a confused mumble of voices from the bedroom, then Sybil's disentangled itself and cried, 'Guests! Why? Who?'

'Bridge guests,' said Mrs. Barrelforth. 'I rounded them up for you as a special treat. Thought it would relax you.'

'I'm not sure I ever want to play bridge

again,' said Sybil.

'You'd better play it this once,' said Mrs. Barrelforth. 'It's going to be interesting. Don't bother to dress. It's only our old friends, Squareless and Whattleboot.'

Sybil looked at Tim inquiringly. 'She must have some reason for it,' said Tim. 'She usually does.'

'All right,' sighed Sybil. 'As long as we don't have to dress.'

Tim slipped his feet into slippers and went to get his bathrobe. When he came back, Sybil was wearing a housecoat that reminded him, with a sheepish twinge, of Millie. It was a subject he hoped wouldn't come up again.

Downstairs, Squareless was sitting in an easy chair beside the fire, which crackled pleasantly in the chill afternoon. His face had regained his customary ruddiness, but his grizzled hair was still hidden under the cap of bandages.

Mr. Whittlebait prowled nervously about the room; he looked as if he wanted to get back to his pinochle game and also as if he disapproved of people being in dishabille in the afternoon. He didn't mention it, naturally, but equally naturally, Squareless did.

'A fine thing,' he growled, 'slapping around like that at this time of day.'

'At least,' said Tim, 'I'm not wearing a nightcap.'

'All right,' grunted Squareless. 'I know I look ridiculous. I can't help it.'

'What happened to you, anyway, Mr. Squareless?' asked Mr. Whittlebait with polite concern. 'I heard you wasn't well.'

'Had a nasty fall,' said Squareless. 'Are we going to play bridge or gossip all afternoon?'

'I'd sort of hoped we were going to have a drink all round,' said Mrs. Barrelforth. 'I'll fix 'em. You folks go ahead with your game.'

Tim set up the card table in front of Squareless, who said he didn't propose to do any moving about. They cut for partners as usual, Sybil drawing Mr. Whittlebait, and settled comfortably to the deal.

Mrs. Barrelforth came back with drinks, passed them around, and stood behind Sybil, watching the play and humming lightly, as if amused by something.

'Do you have to hum?' asked Squareless.

'Sorry,' said Mrs. Barrelforth. She wandered idly to the window and looked out. Tim, glancing up, got the impression she was waiting for something. Apparently she was gazing toward the inlet and the bridge. Whatever she expected, she seemed to be satisfied because she walked back to the table again.

Mr. Whittlebait was struggling meekly with a four-spade contract. On the last nick, he laid down the jack of trumps with a pleased smile that changed to apology as Squareless took it with the queen.

'Thunderation,' he sighed. 'There I go figurin' on that right bower again. Dang!'

'Dang is right, Whattleboot,' said Mrs. Barrelforth cheerfully. 'Even I could see how you had to hold yourself in on that one.'

'Name's Whittlebait, ma'am. Don't know what you mean.'

'The name,' said Mrs. Barrelforth, 'is Frankie Heinkel. I might add that it's been a real pleasure to watch one of the slickest card sharps this side of hell trying to pretend he's a beginner.'

In the silent room, the fire was loud, the thud of the ocean outside thunderous.

'You must be crazy, ma'am,' said Elias Whittlebait.

Mrs. Barrelforth produced two items from her bag. One was a set of handcuffs, the other a revolver which she pointed casually at the handyman.

'You're under arrest, Heinkel,' she said. 'For any number of things. For the murder of Sam Magruder. For the attempted murder of John Squareless. For the murder, seven years ago, of Magruder's British partner, who happens to have been your hostess's father.'

Mr. Whittlebait sat motionless. But his pale eyes glittered behind the thick lenses.

'Dirtiest trick of all, Heinkel,' Mrs. Barrelforth went on, 'was holding out on the message that the man you were about to kill wanted sent to his daughter. You're going to burn, and you're getting off too damned easy.'

Swiftly, so swiftly his hands scarcely

seemed to move, the handyman sent the card table forward with a lunge and followed it with his body, using the overturned table as a shield. From his pocket came a gun. He and Mrs. Barrelforth fired simultaneously, both shots ripping through the table top.

With a little cry of pain and vexation, Mrs. Barrelforth let her revolver fall to the door. Blood appeared on her grotesquely dangling hand.

Tim wasn't aware of making any decision. It seemed natural and automatic that he should be diving for the slight figure crouched between the table legs. His mind, in fact, felt disassociated from his body, watching his hand grope with agonizing uncertainty for the gunman's wrist as a football spectator watches the recovery of a fumble. Then he had the wrist firmly clutched, and their bodies closed in and they rolled over together on the hearthrug.

Tim had weight on his side, but the other's slightness quickly proved to be a rapier wiriness. He twisted and turned like a steel-plated eel. The wrist in Tim's fingers jerked like a piston.

Mrs. Barrelforth had picked up her revolver with her left hand and stood there holding it awkwardly as the two men grappled in a slithering confusion of arms and legs. Sybil pressed her fist to her mouth. Squareless was trying to lift himself from his chair, cursing his impotence.

The wrist slipped out of Tim's fingers, their hands clasped together over small metallic life and death, and the gun went off. In the shattering instant, Tim was sure it was all over for himself. Then, slowly, he realized he was still in one piece, and the writhing eel in his arms was growing limp. Cautiously, suspiciously, he relaxed his hold. Nothing happened, and he stood up. The bullet had torn through the other man's head, and he lay dead in front of the fire.

34

Grand Slam, Redoubled

Sybil swayed against Tim, sobbing in relief. Squareless sank back into his chair, breathing hard. Mrs. Barrelforth was wrapping a handkerchief around her hand and muttering to herself. Then she glanced toward Tim and said, 'Nice work, son. Saved the day. Are you all right?'

'Just scared,' said Tim. 'How about you?'

'Slightly scraped. Not to mention humiliated. Particularly as it was my own bright idea to separate Heinkel from the rest of his gang so I could handle him myself. Instead of which, he damned near handled me.'

'Where is the rest of his gang?' asked Tim.

'In the pokey, I trust. Did you hear that motorcycle go across the bridge a while ago? That was a state trooper giving me the high sign that the hideout had been raided. I don't suppose they put up much of a scrap without Frankie. Which was one reason for getting him out of the way.'

'Where was the hideout?'

'That general store back in the pines. The yokels who sat around the stove there were simply the Heinkel outfit. Apparently the idea of holing up and passing off as a simple-minded back-woods community goes back to the days when Heinkel ran the big casino down the coast. The few genuine Pinies who lived around there were either paid off or terrorized into keeping their traps shut.'

'Did you know all this last night?' asked Tim.

'No,' said Mrs. Barrelforth. 'To tell you the truth, I thought they were using Squareless's house. You remember that Lady Sybil — I'm in the habit of that now, sorry — picked up the same sort of paper there that that inquest note was written on. Turns out it came from the general store. Furthermore, I thought it possible that Lady Sybil had spotted Squareless as Heinkel and that she was the one who took the potshot at him.'

'A similar thought occurred to me,' said Squareless.

'So you told me,' said Sybil. 'And my feelings are still hurt.'

'At that time,' said Squareless, 'I thought you a much more ruthless adventuress than you've turned out to be.'

'But why did Whittlebait or Heinkel, or whoever he is, want to shoot Mr. Squareless?' asked Tim.

'It wasn't Frankie in person,' said Mrs. Barrelforth. 'That cowardly scum never did his own killing. But I don't know, either, why he wanted Squareless knocked off.'

'I think I do,' said Squareless. 'Remember the day when he just couldn't resist that Vienna coup? He thought I'd tumbled to him. He gave me credit, I'm afraid, for being a faster thinker than I am. The truth of the matter didn't dawn on me until today, when Mrs. Barrelforth and I got to talking things over.'

Tim looked at Mrs. Barrelforth. 'Might I ask,' he said, 'if matters of this sort are frequently dealt with by the British-American War Brides Improvement Association?'

Mrs. Barrelforth blew on the fingernails of her left hand. 'It was quite an organization while it lasted,' she said. 'Bit of a feat, really, when you consider that I was the only member.'

'You mean you made it up?' asked Sybil in awe.

'Yep,' said Mrs. Barrelforth. 'I had to invent some pose that would cover a big horse of a lady cop like myself. And I must say the Association worked out very well. Especially the New Jersey chapter.'

Sybil stared. 'Lady cop?'

'One of Scotland Yard's best, my dear,' said Mrs. Barrelforth. 'You should be quite flattered that I was put on your trail. Although, mind you, I wasn't assigned to the States just for that. You see, the Yard has been working pretty closely with the American authorities to break up these ship gambling mobs before they could get their post-war operations under way. Then, when the daughter of a pre-war British operator — forgive me, child, but there it is — turned up as a war bride, I was ordered to stick with her at least until we knew what she was up to. Hence the

Association, which I trusted would enable me to string along as an amiable nuisance.'

'And Sam Magruder?' asked Sybil.

'Sam, my dear, offered his services to the police the day after your father was killed. You're aware, I suppose, that Sam and your father were partners for many years and, to give 'em their due, they were honest as professional gamblers go. The year before the war, this mobster Heinkel, who was already cutting into most landlubbers' gambling, got the bright notion of organizing shipboard professionals into a ring. The idea was that he'd collect all proceeds and pay off as he saw fit. In return, he'd look after 'em if they got into trouble — get lawyers, fix cops, and so on. Anybody who didn't care to join was welcome to the rosy expectation of being shoved overboard. Magruder and your father tried to hold out against him. Finally Magruder saw the writing on the wall and gave in. Then he asked your father to come to New York and talk it over. Your father came, but his mind was made up. Maybe that unhappy scene with you shortly before had something to do with it. Anyway, your father had an interview with Heinkel and Magruder. He was killed an hour later.

'Magruder quit Heinkel cold and Frankie had been gunning for him ever since. The war broke loose, then, and shipboard gambling went to pot. Although from what I hear of GI crap games, more than chocolate bars changed hands. Anyway, during the next few years, Heinkel was too busy dodging the draft to worry about Magruder, and the police had no particular need for Sam then, either. It's only in the past year that all concerned started to pick up where they'd left off.

'Any more questions? If there are, I'd like a drink.'

'Only one,' said Sybil in a small voice. 'With Heinkel dead, and Sam Magruder dead, does anybody — could anybody — know what Daddy's message was?'

Mrs. Barrelforth shook her head, sadly and sympathetically.

There was a stirring and a rumbling from the easy chair where Squareless sat. 'I may be able to throw some light on the matter,' he said. 'You see, I knew Sam Magruder for a great many years. Perhaps you've guessed, Lady Sybil — damn, I've got the habit, too — that I also knew the late self-styled earl.'

Sybil stared at him, her breath coming in short gasps. 'No,' she said. 'I never guessed.'

'Well, I did,' said Squareless. 'Knew him damned well. Knew him too damned well for my own good. I was perfectly aware he made a living at cards, but I had the egotistical notion I could beat him if I kept at it long enough. He was an engaging sort of rascal, too, and it was fun to play with him. If you can call it fun to lose every cent you've got with you in the middle of the Indian Ocean.'

He paused and his beefy hands gripped the arms of the chair. 'Furthermore,' he went on, 'I wasn't alone. You'll recall my telling you, Lady Sybil, that after my wife died in childbirth, I took the unfortunate offspring with me on my travels, with Julia to look after her. You'll also recall my telling you that I lost the child. I lost her, all right. I lost her at sixty-four-card bezique to the man you learned to call your father.' He clamped his lips shut and sank back in his chair. 'God forgive me,' he muttered, but to no one in the room.

There was a long silence. Outside, the light was fading and the wind shook the house.

Sybil went to Squareless's chair and knelt beside him, resting head and elbows on his knees. His hand touched her dark hair, then drew back.

'So you are my father,' she said softly.

'Yes,' said Squareless. 'That's why I arranged with Magruder for you to come here. I thought that perhaps — if we saw a bit of each other — I might get the courage to tell you. I even let myself hope that, given time, you might learn to love me a little.'

'But I do,' whispered Sybil. 'I already do. I did when I met you and I didn't know why. It frightened me. Like Trilby and Svengali.'

'I'm still a little frightened,' said Tim. 'Everybody's turning out to be somebody else except me. Here I am, the same old pedant I always was.'

'You're a lovely pedant, darling,' said Sybil, turning toward him. 'And you've got a lovely father-in-law. I'd be the happiest girl in the world if we only had a lovely fourth for bridge.'

'Patience,' said Tim. 'One of these days . . .'

'Speaking of patience,' said Mrs. Barrelforth, 'did I, or didn't I, ask for a drink a good ten minutes ago?'